BLOODY
SADDLES

Also by L. P. Holmes
in Large Print:

Apache Desert
Brandon's Empire
The Distant Vengeance
Flame of Sunset
High Starlight
Night Marshal
The Plunders
Rustler's Moon
Somewhere They Die

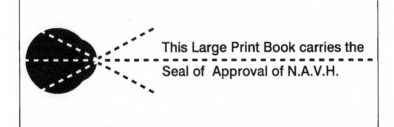

This Large Print Book carries the
Seal of Approval of N.A.V.H.

BLOODY SADDLES

L. P. Holmes

Thorndike Press • Waterville, Maine

Published in 2002 by arrangement with
Golden West Literary Agency.

Thorndike Press Large Print Western Series.

The tree indicium is a trademark of Thorndike Press.

The text of this Large Print edition is unabridged.
Other aspects of the book may vary from the original edition.

Set in 16 pt. Plantin by Minnie B. Raven.

Printed in the United States on permanent paper.

Library of Congress Cataloging-in-Publication Data

Holmes, L. P. (Llewellyn Perry), 1895–
    Bloody saddles / by L.P. Holmes.
        p. cm.
    "Complete and unabridged."
    ISBN 0-7862-3984-0 (lg. print : hc : alk. paper)
    1. Judicial error — Fiction.   2. Ranch life — Fiction.
    3. Escapes — Fiction.   4. Large type books.   I. Title.
    PS3515.O4448 B57 2002
    813′.52—dc21   2001054084

BLOODY
SADDLES

CHAPTER ONE

Judge Henning finished speaking. Buck Comstock, having stood up to receive his sentence, surveyed the Judge with cool, sardonic, contemptuous eyes. He even smiled slightly, a set and savage expression to mask the cold rigor which seemed to congeal his blood and freeze his heart. Twenty-five years . . . !

Judge Henning would not meet Buck's eyes. At no time during the trial had he met Buck's eyes. And as he rendered sentence, his glance had been past Buck, over his head. For a long second after the droning voice of the Judge died away, the courtroom was dead still, so still that when old Bill Morgan cleared his throat wrathfully, the sound was like a thunder clap.

Sheriff Brood Shotwell stepped up and took Buck by the right arm. Spike St. Ives, Shotwell's number one deputy, moved up on the other side. "That's that," growled Brood Shotwell. "Come on, Comstock."

Buck shrugged, turned and walked between the two of them toward the side door of the court room, a door which opened to a space of some ten yards of outdoors, beyond which stood the waiting jail. Buck turned his head and looked out over the crowd in the court room. He saw Bill Morgan and Johnny Frazier and Bud Tharp pushing their way along as though to intercept Buck and his two guards before they could reach that side door. The intent of these faithful three was plain in their eyes and attitude.

"No go, Bill," called Buck sharply. "It wouldn't work, anyhow. Don't start anything."

"I'll try not to, Buck," answered Bill Morgan. "But I want to state right here and now that of all the cheap, crooked, low down farces ever pulled under the name of the law — this is the worst. I thought that damned, squint-eyed old rooster up there was a judge."

Everybody in that room heard Bill. He spoke as he usually did, in rumbling tones which would carry a hundred yards in the teeth of a high wind. Judge Henning's pursy mouth tightened. He whanged his gavel on his desk.

"There will be no remarks against the

dignity of this court," he shrilled. "I'll have you cited for contempt. Sheriff, remove your prisoner."

"That's the right word," bellowed Bill Morgan. "Contempt — I got plenty of that for you and all the rest of the mealy mouthed crowd connected with this travesty. And you just try and cite me for anything, you weasel-eyed old buzzard. Try and have me arrested for this or that or anything else you can think up in that peanut, twisted, buckshot article you call your brain. Yeah, go ahead. Just try and have me arrested. I'm in a shooting frame of mind right now and the first hombre that touches me gets frazzled out to a plumb worthless fringe. That's cold turkey. Eat it or choke over it, whichever you please."

"Bill!" yelled Buck. "Will you shut up!"

Bill Morgan subsided with a growl. There was a lot of talk going on among the other spectators in the court room now. Some there were who seemed angry at Bill — others were nodding their heads in commendation of his stand. A tipsy puncher, standing just inside the main door of the court room, yipped shrilly.

"That's telling 'em, you old juniper. 'N if you need any help at smoke rollin', just

9

you call on lil' Smoky Rawlins. He'll be with you — till hell freezes. Yes sir — that's me — Smoky Rawlins. And I don't like judges — or sheriffs — one damn little bit better than you do."

This brought a laugh from many in the crowd and the tension lessened. Buck, realizing that neither Bill nor Johnny Frazier nor Bud Tharp would do anything foolish or reckless now, turned his head and let his gaze fix on Leek Jaeger and Frank Cutts, who stood near that side door.

Leek Jaeger, squat and burly, was rocking back and forth on his heels and toes, a habit of his when particularly pleased over something. His blocky, heavily jowled face, perennially unshaven, was drawn to a mocking grin, while his eyes, little and deep set, and of the dull, brutal color of old lead, were squinted with triumph.

Frank Cutts was Jaeger's partner. An ex-gambler, Cutts still affected the immaculate, somberly dandified dress of his former calling. He had a thin, pale, graven mask of a face, expressionless in all but his eyes. These were sharp and black and held the same glinting triumph which showed in the dull orbs of his partner.

Buck Comstock's glance went over the

two men swiftly and came to rest on the girl who stood between them. Buck had been wondering about that girl. Though the trial had dragged through the better part of two weeks and though Jaeger and Cutts had been present every day, this had been the first appearance of the girl. She had come in on this day of sentence and had sat between the two men throughout the proceedings. Buck had spied her the moment she set foot in the courtroom and had wondered, a lot.

Who was she — and what was a girl of her evident high class doing with a pair of whelps like Jaeger and Cutts? Buck would have given a lot to know. For she was a definitely pretty girl, not over twenty or twenty-one years of age, a girl with wide, grave, dusky eyes, crisp black hair and a softly crimson mouth. Her skin was of a remarkably pure, richly tinted old ivory. Yes, a mighty pretty girl, this slim young person. Not the baby faced kind of prettiness — but beauty that had depth and dignity, and mental alertness and poise.

Slim she was, trig and dainty in a close fitting traveling suit of some kind of dark brown material with a little trick of a hat perched on her dusky head. Buck had never seen a girl just like her before. Obviously she was not a native to this range country.

Just before Buck and his two guards came opposite the little group, Leek Jaeger leaned over and murmured something in the girl's ear. Her eyes sought Buck's face and she seemed to shrink slightly, with the same expression of revulsion she might have shown had she looked at a rattle-snake, or a feral, murderous wolf. The implication of that shudder brought the hot blood burning up under the sun-blackened tan of Buck's throat and lean, clean set jaw. But he met her glance squarely and coolly. Then Brood Shotwell kicked that side door open and Buck was outside, under the shade of a clump of cottonwoods.

Buck would have liked to linger a bit under those cottonwoods. Where he was going there wouldn't be any. And until now, Buck had never realized what beauty and majesty there was, even in a gnarled old cottonwood. How cool and green the leaves were, and how rich the music in their soft fluttering before the push of the lazy afternoon wind! And the trunks and the limbs of the trees — there was a certain clean, staunch vitality about them, somehow. Up there, on a nodding branch tip, gay in black and gold, an oriole balanced and poured wild, sweet music from a swelling throat. Buck weaved a little bit, suddenly dizzy with strangled emotion. From this — to twenty-five years in Pinole — !

"Hurry up," rasped Brood Shotwell. "I want to get you safe behind the bars again, Comstock. Some of those salty pals of yours, like that tough old hairpin, Bill Morgan, might get wild notions if we stand out here in the open too long."

Two more steps and the jail door clanged shut behind Buck. The jar of it rang in his ears like a sombre bell tolling the death march. He stumbled over to the hard, comfortless, solitary bunk and sat down, his head dropping into his hands.

Twenty-five years! He could hear Judge Henning saying those fateful words again, rolling them over his lisping lips, in that precise, perfect diction which the old devil affected. Twenty-five years! A quarter of a century — a lifetime to one who was young and full of the turbulent energy which the wide, wild range gives to its sons. Twenty-five years behind stone walls, behind iron bars — deadly confinement, brutal isolation where even the comfort of the stars was denied a man. He'd never live through it. Buck Comstock knew that. Cage an eagle — and kill it. An old truth. Freedom, to all things which had always known it, was the most precious elixir of life. With it gone — all was gone. . . .

Buck shook his head savagely. He had to get a grip on himself. He had to show Jaeger and Cutts and their ilk, that though they might get him down, they couldn't whip him. If there was only something of real substance he could fight! That was the hellish part of a thing like this. It overpowered a man, beat him down. You couldn't get your hands on it, to rip and pound and tear. You couldn't look it over through smoke. It was too big, too intangible. It was a system, ponderous, slow-moving, but certain. And those in the know could use that system to serve their own unholy, scheming ends. Like Cutts and Jaeger.

Buck began pacing up and down, cursing bitterly. He was not given over to much profanity aside from an occasional mild cuss word. But now — he had to have some outlet to the agony of impotence which racked him. He grabbed the bars in one of the windows, shook them savagely.

Abruptly he quieted, went back to the bunk and sat down, thumbed a thin sack of tobacco from his shirt pocket and built a smoke. He inhaled deeply, and the tangy smoke soothed and quieted his scrambled nerves. He had to hold in — take this like a man.

Keys jangled at the jail door and the portal of heartbreak opened. It was Brood Shotwell and Curt Wallace who came in. Curt Wallace stood looking miserably at Buck. A slender young chap in store clothes, Curt had a sensitive face, which was now wreathed in gloom.

"Buck," he said, "this is hell. I don't know what to say. It's all my fault. I made a mess of things. As a lawyer, I'd make a good sheep-herder."

Buck shook his head. "Not your fault, Curt. You did everything any man could do. In the face of the way Jaeger and Cutts had things fixed and stacked against me, the greatest lawyer in the world would have been helpless. No — not your fault. Forget it."

"Forget it!" exploded Curt. "I'll never be able to forget it — not as long as I live. Twenty-five years in Pinole! Good Lord! Buck, do you realize what that means?"

Buck's smile was bitter, harsh. "Reckon I do, Curt. That sentence was equivalent to a rope around my neck — only I'll be a damn site longer dying. Twenty-five years —. A long time, Curt — too long. And did you see how old Henning enjoyed passing that sentence? He shore rolled those words over his tongue like he loved 'em."

"Listen," growled Brood Shotwell. "I'm not supposed to stand here while you jaspers run down Judge Henning, you know. If you got business to go over, get about it. But lay off throwing mud at Henning and his court. I don't like it."

Buck laughed softly, but there was a harsh sound in that laugh, like the breaking of brittle ice. "If you stick around me, Brood — you'll have to listen. Henning is a shyster, with a rotten mark on his soul. And he's not alone."

Brood Shotwell's heavy brows drew down. "Meaning what — by that crack?"

"You figure it out, Brood. You always had a pretty good head on your shoulders. Just you put two and two together and see where it leads. Curt, wipe that gloom off your phiz. You did your best — and that's all any angel can do."

"I'm going to keep on fighting, of course," declared Curt Wallace stubbornly. "If I have to, I'll go clear to the Governor."

Buck shrugged wearily. "Doubt if it would do a mite of good, Curt. Besides, my money is about gone. I'm just about broke."

16

"Damn the money," cried Wallace. "This is for principle — and friendship. Buck, they framed you — railroaded you. I'm not what you'd call exactly old, but I've seen a fair amount of court procedure, and if there was ever a farce and a travesty of justice — this was it. Bill Morgan was more than right there."

Sheriff Brood Shotwell looked at his watch. "I ain't got time to stand around here while you jaspers talk in circles. If you got anything real important to say — get it off your chests — and then Wallace and I'll get out of here. I got to make arrangements to start Comstock traveling towards Pinole — first thing tomorrow morning."

Young Curt Wallace steadied to a grave dignity. "Somewhere in this mess are filthy fingers and lying tongues — also, some crooked motives. I'm sticking with the proposition until I uncover some of those things. When I do, this country is going to see a shake-down they'll date time from." He shook hands with Buck. "Keep your chin up, old timer. Twenty-five years is a long time for a flock of snakes to keep entirely out of sight. And I'll be waiting with a club for the first head that shows."

They went out, the door closed, and Buck was once more alone. Suddenly it

17

swept over him — just how much alone. Beyond those four mocking walls he had some friends — but there was nothing they could do. This thing was about settled. Twenty-five years! Buck's self control began to slip and he got hold of it savagely.

If he lived those twenty-five years through he would be over fifty when he got out. Over fifty — an old man, with all the best of his life gone by. All his hard work, his ambitions, his purpose in life shot to hell — thrown away — wasted. And all because of muddy hate, crooked hearts, and lying tongues.

Buck knew how a trapped animal felt. And now that it was all over, somehow the whole scene lay fairly clear before him. Looking back, he could see how cunningly the net had been woven, how it had been folded and drawn about him until there wasn't a loop-hole left for him. And he knew that as long as he lived he would never forget the look of satisfaction on the faces of Leek Jaeger and Frank Cutts as he passed them on his way out of the court-room.

Then there was that girl. What would a girl like her be doing around such as those two coyotes? She looked so clean and fine and proud — so far above anything connected with anything mean and crooked. Buck could see her almost, as she stood there. But he recalled the glance of aversion and loathing she had thrown at him, and the clear vision of her faded. Buck's eyes clouded with bitterness and loneliness.

The afternoon waned and died. Dusk came in and the shadows in the jail thickened to blackness. Through the narrow, barred windows, Buck could see the stars winking out. He had always liked to watch the stars. Many a night he had lain in his soogan roll, looking up at them, watching them slow wheel and march, thinking thoughts which didn't particularly make hard, practical sense, but which somehow lifted a man up. There wouldn't be any stars in Pinole. Even their ageless brilliance could not penetrate stone walls — prison walls.

Deputy Spike St. Ives came in with Buck's supper. He carried a tray in one hand, a ready gun in the other. From the crook of his left arm hung a lantern. A lanky, cadaverous sort of a man, Spike St. Ives. He had a narrow, hard face crowned with a rusty mop of hair. St. Ives often snarled, but never smiled. When sent out to round up a prisoner, Spike St. Ives was known to prefer to shoot first and consider arrest later. A hard man — a tough one.

Buck, forestalling the deputy's usual command, moved over into a far corner, while St. Ives deposited lantern and tray of food on the bunk. Then St. Ives retreated to the door while Buck crossed to the bunk and began his supper.

"Looks like this is the last night you'll have to bother with me, Spike," drawled Buck casually.

St. Ives grunted. "Damned glad of it. I never did like to wet nurse a killer."

Buck's eyes narrowed. But he said nothing more. You got nowhere arguing with a jasper like Spike St. Ives. The man lacked all sense of humor, in fact, he seemed to lack about all human sentiments except a hard, savage, brutal tenacity for his job. Maybe as a deputy sheriff St. Ives was mighty efficient. Only, thought Buck sardonically, it was strange to be called a killer by a man who packed no less than seven notches on his guns.

When Buck finished with his meal, St. Ives gathered up the dishes and went out. Buck built a smoke and went over to a window. Here he could pick up the murmur of the town.

Twin Buttes was a pretty sizable cow

town, being the county seat as well as feeding a big range. Buck could visualize the street at this time of night. There would be quite a few riders in by this time, more in fact than usual, for they would want to know all the news about the trial from those luckier ones who had been present. They'd be grouped in little knots up and down the board side-walks, arguing. The Yellow Horse saloon would be doing a rushing business. Yeah, the old town would be pretty lively tonight.

A spur chain tinkled softly somewhere near by, and Buck stiffened slightly. Then a low, rumbling call reached him. "Hey — Buck! Oh Buck!"

Buck grinned. "Hello, Bill," he answered. "Don't bust a gallus trying to keep that bull-bass voice of yours pulled down to a whisper."

Three dim figures moved up outside the window, Bill Morgan, Johnny Frazier and Bud Tharp. "How you doing, Buck?" asked Bill.

"Well, they feed me regular and if it wasn't that I was thinking so much about what twenty-five years in Pinole will mean, I'd be pretty well off."

Bill swore soulfully. "You're not going to Pinole, boy — don't you ever think it.

21

Sometime between now and daylight, Johnny and Bud and me — we're going to tear this damn calaboose plumb apart at the hinges. We've all sent out to our spreads for our outfits and when they show up, we'll start the fire-works. We'll show Jaeger and Cutts and that old rat of a Judge Henning if they can put over a farce like this on a friend of ours. Yes sir, we're going to bust you loose and if Brood Shotwell tries to stop us, we'll bust him, too."

"No you won't," said Buck quietly. "I'm shore thanking you boys for the sentiments behind those words, but I won't stand for you letting yourselves in for a lot of trouble over me. You hear?"

"It won't be trouble, Buck," drawled Johnny Frazier. "It'll be fun. Just imagine how Henning will squall. And Jaeger — he'll be fit to tie. Shucks! We ain't the kind of friends to let you down in a spot like this."

"You're three lunk headed idiots," growled Buck, trying to keep the emotion he felt out of his voice. "I won't have it, I tell you."

"You got nothing to say about it," rumbled Bill Morgan. "You just lay low and keep your shirt on. Long about midnight this jail is going to be caved — complete."

Now a harsh snarling voice bit in from the darkness — Spike St. Ives' voice. "What's going on over there? Who the hell is at that window?"

"What's it to you, you sour-phizzed star toter," retorted Bill Morgan truculently. "This is Johnny Frazier, Bud Tharp and me — Bill Morgan. We're having a little talk with Buck Comstock. And if you don't like it — what are you going to do about it?"

Buck heard St. Ives curse, then saw his gangling figure come slithering up through the gloom. "Get away from that window," rasped the deputy. "There'll be no jail delivery of that prisoner — or slipping a gun to him through those bars. Get traveling I said."

But Tharp answered him. Bud was a quiet, slow talking sort, easy to get along with, but a regular buzz-saw when on the peck. Most men listened when that crisp note came into Bud Tharp's voice.

"Listen, St. Ives — to some folks you may be a big, bad sidewinder. But to Bill and Johnny and me, you're just a pot of sour milk with all the cream of human decency skimmed off. This ground we're standing on is public property. If you think you can move us off, come arunning, or ashooting — whichever way appeals to you."

St. Ives slowed down. Bill Morgan, Johnny Frazier and Bud Tharp were solid, substantial citizens on the Twin Buttes range. They owned ranches and ran pretty sizable spreads. They had a lot of friends. In addition, they were fighting men in their own right. They couldn't be bluffed or scared. And St. Ives knew that if he tried to throw a gun on them he'd be shot to tatters in jig time. He mollified his attitude.

"If you want to talk to Comstock, you could say so at the office and we'd let you in regular," he blurted.

"We're not asking any favors of you or Shotwell either," retorted Bud Tharp crisply. "After seeing the kind of deal that was put over on Buck, we ain't exactly what you'd call trustful or full of respect for any so-called force of the law in this neck of the woods. Speaking personal and right to the point, I think you're all a bunch of gol blasted crooks. So what?"

"I'll go get Brood and see what he has to say about that," snarled St. Ives, slouching away.

Bill Morgan snorted his disgust and turned back to the matter at hand. "You be ready, Buck," he said. "We're going to cave this jail in and nothing is going to stop us. You be waiting for us."

"I wish you jaspers would listen to reason," argued Buck. "You'll only stir up a big jag of trouble for yourselves. Shotwell and St. Ives may be anything you want to call 'em — but you can stick a pin in this. They won't give me up without a fight. There'll he shooting and somebody will get killed. And I don't want anybody killed over me. Curt Wallace said he wasn't done fighting yet, not by a jug-full. Curt said —."

"Curt Wallace had his chance in that so-called court of law," rumbled Morgan. "He didn't get results. So Johnny and Bud and me are going to try our hand. We got to be moving. Our boys will be showing up any time now, and we don't want them to start taking things apart in the wrong direction. Remember, you be ready — and we'll be seeing you later, cowboy."

They jingled off, these three sturdy, staunch friends, and Buck strained his eyes after them until they vanished in the dark. He wondered at the thickness in his throat. They had so much to lose and so little to gain by this move they were planning to make. Yet, for a friend they were eager and willing and determined to throw everything into the pot and let it ride.

Again three figures showed as shadows in the gloom. For a moment Buck thought it was his three friends coming back. But he soon knew differently as he identified St. Ives' snarling voice. They paused for a moment at the jail door, too much at an angle for Buck to watch them. He saw a yellow glow leap up as a lantern was lighted. Then keys rattled, a lock snicked and the door opened with a bang and Brood Shotwell and Spike St. Ives stepped in, both with drawn guns. Behind them, holding the lantern high, was Leek Jaeger.

"We want that gun that Morgan or one of the other two slipped you, Comstock," grated Shotwell. "Where is it?"

Buck shrugged and smiled faintly. "They slipped me no gun," he said. "I know you won't believe that, so you can start searching."

They did search, first going over him, then rooting all through the bunk. "You see?" said Buck mockingly.

St. Ives would have answered him savagely, but Brood Shotwell cut him short. "All right, Spike," growled the sheriff. "You can ram along. Go out to Long Barn and see if you can locate that Mex vaquero

26

— the one they call Concho. Slim Bradley swears that Concho knows where that Oregon bronc of Slim's went to. Bring the Mex in if you can find him. I want to question him, though, privately. I think Slim was too drunk to know who did steal his horse."

St. Ives hesitated. "Suppose Morgan and that crowd try a jail delivery. You'll need help."

Shotwell laughed curtly. "I've never had a prisoner taken from me yet. Get going."

St. Ives shrugged and went out, leaving Shotwell and Leek Jaeger there, looking at Buck. Sitting on the edge of the bunk, Buck was strung tight and cold. He never imagined that he could hate any man like he hated Leek Jaeger. Even in that tumultuous moment when he had faced Ben Sloan through smoke, he had not known hate, or anything remotely approaching it. He had gone for his gun and turned lead loose on Sloan merely because of the instinctive prompting of the oldest unwritten law in the world — the law of self-preservation. But he had not known hate.

With Leek Jaeger it was different. From the very moment he had first laid eyes on Jaeger, some two years before, he had hated the man. It was something instinctive, something which had leaped into life, full blown and savage, with the first meeting of their eyes. And that hate had grown with the years. Now, in view of what had happened in the past few weeks it was like a bitter, consuming fire. Buck spoke to Brood Shotwell, his voice dry and bleak.

"If you've brought that Jaeger pole-cat in here so he can gloat, Brood — you're less of a man that I ever thought you'd be."

"I didn't bring him in here for that reason," growled Shotwell. "He's got something to tell you — some kind of a proposition to make."

"I want no dealing with him, not of any kind," rasped Buck. "The truth isn't in him. I wouldn't trust him an inch in broad daylight."

"Wait a minute, Comstock," said Jaeger. "I know you hate my guts. That's your privilege and you can bet it's returned, with interest. But I got a proposition to make to you — based entirely on a business viewpoint. You'll be wise to listen to me. Twenty-five years is a long time — a hell of a long time — and you'd be a damn sight bigger fool than I think you are if you aren't willing to make a trade that'll cut that time to maybe — well, say five years. Think that over."

Buck sat very still, his thoughts racing. What was Jaeger up to? What sort of a scheme was going on in that bullet head? What sort of a trade could Jaeger possibly manipulate which would reduce that sentence from twenty-five to five years? And why was he offering it?

Buck's first impulse was to tell Jaeger to go to hell. This fellow was as tricky a sidewinder as ever came down the pike. And Buck felt that he would rather spend a lifetime in Pinole, than truckle in any way to this man he hated so savagely. But he choked back what he felt, for he realized it wouldn't hurt matters a bit to get some inkling as to what was on Jaeger's mind. Buck fenced cautiously.

"You're just making talk, Jaeger. You may figure that you're the he-wolf in this neck of the woods, but you don't rate big enough to cut any part of that sentence."

"I wouldn't be here tonight if I wasn't sure of my ground," said Jaeger curtly. "If you want to listen to that proposition, say so without any more lally-gagging around. Otherwise I'll be on my way."

Buck stood up, began pacing back and forth across the inner end of the cell. His thoughts were stabbing in all directions, trying to pick up a hint as to what was in

Jaeger's mind, and what was behind this visit. Maybe Jaeger was worried with the idea that Bill Morgan and the other boys might actually bring about a jail delivery, and what such a delivery might lead to. Or maybe —. Another thought came to Buck, a thought which sent the quick, white flame of hope burning through him.

Buck's eyes, narrowed and hidden by the shadows which lay above the ragged circle of light thrown by the lantern, were burning with a strange and reckless light. If Leek Jaeger could in any way reverse that twenty-five year sentence, it was an unconscious admission that the whole trial was indeed a railroad set-up and that Jaeger was more than a little afraid of events which might be uncovered in the future. Buck shrugged. "All right," he snapped. "Let's hear what you have to offer, Jaeger."

Jaeger produced a black cheroot, gnawed the end off it, spat noisily and lit the smoke. He roiled it leisurely back and forth in his ugly lips, making a repulsive, smacking noise. "I won't mince words," he said finally. "I can use that Cotton Valley range of yours, Comstock. With you heading for Pinole tomorrow, I could go ahead and grab it, regardless. That would raise quite a stink, of course, but I reckon I could live it down. I've made quite a jag of folks take it and like it, before this. Still and all, I don't like trouble any more than the next man, so I'm willing to make a bargain with you. Sign that Cotton Valley range over to me and I'll see that twenty years are taken off that sentence. There it is — straight up and down. Take it or leave it."

Buck resumed his pacing, his thoughts flying. Plain it was, now — all of it. The trial and everything. Jaeger wanted his range. To get it he'd push a charge and manipulate a supposedly fair court of law to send a man to jail for a quarter of a century. Yet, because of hidden things which might jump up at any time about that trial and backfire, Jaeger would still pull strings, still smear on more of his dirty work, in an effort to get that Cotton Valley range and at the same time cover up his tracks as much as possible.

A gust of night wind soughed plaintively around the jail. The door creaked slightly. Deep fire glowed in Buck Comstock's eyes. He glanced at Brood Shotwell — at Jaeger, wondering if they had noted that creaking door. For that door was not locked!

Brood Shotwell was staring frowningly at the floor. Jaeger, complacence and confidence on his blocky face was watching the tobacco smoke curl before him. Savage and relentless decision gripped Buck.

"And after I signed over that Cotton Valley range — what's to prevent you from letting me be dragged off to Pinole and then forgetting all about me?" Buck demanded.

Jaeger shrugged. "You'll just have to take my word for that."

Brood Shotwell stirred restlessly and spoke. "Maybe you don't realize it, Leek — but the talk you've made right here and now throws a nasty smell over my office, over Judge Henning and over the whole organization of law and order on Twin Buttes range. Me — I don't like it — not one little bit."

"You'll have to lump it then, Shotwell," said Jaeger bluntly. "Let me see — three months from now you come up for election, don't you? Kind of like your job, eh Brood? Well, go out and see who controls the votes in Twin Buttes County. You'll find out that I do. If you try and buck me, I'll break you just like I've broken a lot of thick-headed hombres. You sing low, do as you're told, and you'll get along. If you don't — well." Jaeger shrugged and turned to Buck. "You made up your mind, Comstock? Make it fast. I ain't got all night to sit here. What's your answer?"

"This," crackled Buck.

Ten feet clear he covered in one terrific, diving plunge — a long, lean, hurtling projectile. Whipping out ahead of him was a leaden fist, backed by muscles strung to a rawhide power and a cold, surging fury. That whistling fist caught Leek Jaeger squarely in the middle of the face, pulping his nose, mashing his lips, almost crucifying him.

Jaeger, in falling, crashed into Brood Shotwell and the two men went down in a tangle. Buck, already on his way to the door, kicked out at the lantern, which smashed against the bunk. There was a gust of smoke, then a spreading ball of flame, spattering flame, some of which landed on Brood Shotwell's pants leg.

The sheriff, fumbling wildly for his gun, felt the bite of that flame and started slapping madly at it. This split second of delay was all the edge Buck Comstock needed. In another jump he had slammed open the door of the jail, was outside and running.

He whipped about the corner of the old adobe courthouse and darted into the street. A group of saddle mounts were tied to a handy hitch rail. Buck did not hesitate.

This was no time for delicate ethics. He swung into the nearest saddle and lifted the bronco to a wild run.

Down the street he sped, crouched low in the saddle. Those stragglers along the street who took note of the pounding hoofs, could only wonder. It was too dark for them to identify either rider or horse. And cowboys had left town at top speed before this, for perfectly innocent reasons. So, there was no attempt to halt Buck's flying departure.

And by the time Brood Shotwell could put out his burning pants and drag the dazed and bleeding Leek Jaeger out of the spreading flames inside the jail and spread the alarm, Buck Comstock was well clear of the town of Twin Buttes and racing on into the far, free night.

CHAPTER TWO

The Twin Buttes range, aside from a lot of dry and comparatively worthless desert range, well south and away out east, was made up of three distinct and separate valleys, running roughly parallel and radiating from north to south from an area of broken, tangled malpais country, from the center of which rose two jagged, wind and weather scarified buttes. These two buttes, known locally as East Butte and West Butte, were the basis of the name for the county and for the town, which lay at the head of the western valley.

Buck Comstock, speeding out of the southern end of the single street of Twin Buttes, immediately turned east and set the horse he had grabbed to a long, ground eating run. Buck had spent a lifetime in the saddle and he knew horses. This one was a good horse, fresh and full of fire. Somehow it came to him vaguely that he knew this horse, that he recognized its gait, that he had ridden it before. He fingered the horn, passed a hand over the bucking rolls. There, on the face of the rolls was smooth, cold metal, metal set into the leather, metal shaped like a star. And then Buck knew. This was Bill Morgan's horse — Bill's big, bald faced sorrel!

Buck laughed aloud. This was good, plenty good. Chance could not have thrown a better break his way. Maybe it meant that his luck had changed. For one thing was certain. No matter what else might be laid to his door, good old Bill would never accuse him of horse stealing. The fact that Buck had, by pure chance seized upon this bronco for a getaway, would tickle Bill pink. It would make Bill feel that in some way he had contributed to Buck's escape.

Knowing which horse he was up on, Buck had little worry now of being picked up by a stern chase, even if Brood Shotwell did get organized and managed to pick up his trail. For Bill Morgan's bald faced sorrel was known the length and breadth of the Twin Buttes range for its speed and bottom and staying power.

On Buck's left, jagged and lonely against the starlit sky, loomed the bulk of East and West Buttes. Buck reined gradually toward them, with the idea of skirting the malpais country. This would take him well above the J Bar C headquarters, which lay midway across the first, or Timber Valley. Also, that malpais was a good place to be close to in case he bumped into somebody with ideas of stopping him. A fellow could bust into that malpais in a hurry and leave a trail that only the devil and all his dogs could follow.

Under the drumming hoofs of the sorrel the miles rolled swiftly back, and soon the horse was breasting a long, climbing slope, where scattered, stunted sage began to take the place of the grassland of the valley. This slope topped a sort of table land, barren and rocky, where the starlight lay like pale white fire and the wind sang a free and pungent course.

Two miles of this and Buck dropped down into the center valley, wide and flat, and the richest of the three main valleys of the Twin Buttes range. This was Coyote Valley and here lay Bill Morgan's Circle Star spread, Bud Tharp's Rafter T, Johnny Frazier's Lazy F, and far at the southern end, the Stirrup Cross outfit, which belonged to old man Addis.

Beyond the fertile reaches of Coyote Valley and across another sage and juniper tableland, lay Cotton Valley, in the center of which stood Buck's own little spread, the Half Moon. South of Buck's spread Cotton Valley ran out into a lot of free range, government land which lacked water, so that it was only of tangible grazing value in the late winter and spring.

The northern portion of Cotton Valley lay under the control of the Wineglass iron, which had been Ben Sloan's spread. But now that Ben Sloan was dead, it was problematical as to who would eventually own the Wineglass.

Again, before Buck Comstock's eyes a picture took form, a picture which seemed to be carved indelibly on the retina of his mind, a picture he had seen so many, many times during the past month. It was of Ben Sloan, hatchet face set in a killing snarl, eyes red with blood hunger, crouched in deadly belligerence as he dragged at his guns. And then, somehow, Buck's gun had leaped into his hand, coughing heavily in report, jarring and rearing in recoil. And Ben Sloan's pigeon toes had turned still further inward and he had lunged out on his face, the startled wonder of death in his staring eyes.

For that they had called Buck a killer. For that they had dragged him to jail, tried him and sentenced him to twenty-five years in Pinole Penitentiary. Now, however, he was once more free, at least for a time, a fugitive from law, but still — free.

The sorrel halted, heaved a gusty sigh and stood tossing its head. Aroused abruptly from his thoughts, Buck saw before him a corral and the heavy bulk of feed sheds and ranch buildings looming through the dark. Startled for a moment, Buck laughed softly, relaxed and patted the sorrel's neck. The horse had come home. This was the Circle Star, Bill Morgan's spread.

The place was silent, seemingly deserted. Buck recalled that Bill Morgan, Bud Tharp and Johnny Frazier had all sent out to their ranches for their crews, to help in the jail delivery which now would never be consummated. Well, if the Circle Star was deserted, Buck decided he'd help himself to what he needed, for he knew he would be more than welcome to anything which Bill Morgan owned.

And then, as Buck dismounted, he caught the pale gleam of light in a single back window of the ranchhouse. Buck looked back along the way he had come, eyes and ears straining. There was no sound of pursuit, no sight of any moving thing. So he prowled around to the lighted window and peered guardedly in.

A grim smile flickered over his face. In that room, sprawled at ease on his bunk, lay fat, rotund Bones Baker, the Circle Star cook. Bones held a magazine of lurid romance in both tense fists and by the light of the lamp on the chair beside his bunk, was reading avidly.

Buck banged softly on the window. Bones jerked upright, stared around. Buck tapped the window again. Bones unearthed a forty-five Colt from under his blankets, pushed open the window and leaned out.

"Who is it?" he demanded belligerently. "If any of you gol darn grub spoilers are aiming to play a trick on me I'll hash you up with a couple of slugs."

"It's Buck Comstock, Bones," drawled Buck. "Can I come in?"

Bones' jaw dropped, his eyes bugged out. "Huh — huh — who? Buck Comstock? How the hell? Sa—ay, you're supposed to be in the jug."

"I know. But I made a break for it, won free and jumped that big sorrel of Bill's. The bronc brought me straight here. I got to make a hideaway somewhere, Bones. I'll need grub and some blankets — and a

40

couple of guns. How's chances?"

Bones flung the window wide. "Goddle-mighty, boy — you shore can have 'em," he exclaimed. "Climb in here. Gollies, I'm glad to see you. I heard they gave you twenty-five years in Pinole for killing that pigeon toed ole tarantula bug, Ben Sloan. I was feeling plenty bad about that, y'betcha. The outfit all hightailed to town this evening and I heard 'em talking something about a jail delivery. Was they the ones who broke you loose?"

"No. I knew that Bill and Bud and Johnny and all their boys were figuring on something of the sort, but I beat 'em to it."

"Swell!" exulted Bones, as he wrung Buck's hand tightly. "You bet you can have that grub and those blankets. You can have anything on this danged ranch you want. You had any supper?"

"Yeah. I fed before I had my chance for a break. Don't waste no time while you're throwing that pack of blankets and grub together, Bones. Shotwell is pounding along my trail back there somewhere by this time. He'll be shore to end up here eventually and I want to be a long time gone when he gets here."

Bones caught up the lamp and waddled out. In five minutes he had a flour sack of grub and a couple of blankets ready. He made another short journey and came back with a pair of gun belts, heavy with cartridges and holstered weapons. Under the other arm he had a rifle.

"Here y'are," he puffed. "These are Bill's spare belt guns and one of the half dozen or so rifles always cluttering up the house. I'll rustle you some ca'tridges."

Ten minutes after he had first knocked on the window, Buck was ready to leave. In addition to grub, blankets, guns and ammunition, Bones had given him an old sombrero and a short, warm jacket. As a final thought Bones threw in a slicker. Then he helped Buck lug it all down to the corrals.

"Better keep right on traveling on that sorrel, Buck," advised Bones. "Bill won't mind a bit. He kinda thinks a lot of you, cowboy."

"They don't come any better than Bill," said Buck. "But I won't want that sorrel. Known too well in these parts. See if you can find me an old saddle while I catch up some ordinary nag."

Bones got the saddle and Buck cinched it on a well built grullo, an Indian horse carrying a brand no white man could hope to decipher. Buck tied grub, blankets and slicker behind the cantle, slung the rifle in the boot under the stirrup leather, then turned to Bones once more.

"Listen close. I don't want you to forget a word of this, Bones. I want to see Bill. I got to see him. I want to have a long talk with him. But I can't afford the chance of sticking around here. He'll have to come to me. Tell him I'll meet him tomorrow night around midnight at Indian Spring. Don't forget."

"I won't," promised Bones. "How you fixed for money? I got about twenty bucks here you can have."

Buck jabbed the fat cook affectionately in the stomach. "Thanks. I don't need money. I need friends. I got one in you. So long, Bones."

Bones Baker listened until the sound of the grullo's hoofs died away. Then he started automatically to unsaddle the sorrel, but stopped almost immediately.

"Nope," he muttered — "that won't do. Brood Shotwell is liable to come rammin' in here hellity-larrup any old minute and I don't want him to think that Buck was here. I'll just leave this nag stand here as is."

As an after thought he looped the reins

about the saddle horn, knowing the sorrel would stay put there by the corral anyway. Then he went back to the ranchhouse and squatted in the doorway to listen and wait.

A half hour later, coming down on the ranch from the west, was the rising clatter of speeding hoofs. Bones nodded wisely, returned to his room and sprawled out on his bunk once more.

He heard those racing hoofs speed to a halt outside the door, then the clamor of voices, among which he recognized Bill Morgan's heavy rumble, and Brood Shotwell's cold, clipped tones. Then Bill Morgan yelled — "Hey Bones — wake up and come on out here!"

Bones went to the door, magazine in one hand, lamp in the other. He stood in the open doorway, yawning hugely. "Hi, Bill — what'cha want? What's all the excitement about?"

Brood Shotwell stalked up out of the darkness, Bill Morgan behind him. "You been awake all evening?" demanded Shotwell harshly.

"Yeah," nodded Bones. "Been thinkin' of turning in and getting some shut-eye, but this story was so gol darn exciting I couldn't let go of it. You ought to read it, Brood. About a doctor who'd mixed up some kind of poison and went around —."

Shotwell cursed bleakly. "Seen or heard anybody ride in here?" he grated harshly. "Huh?" Bones shook his head. "Not until you jaspers came in. Why? You looking for somebody?"

"Oh, no," growled Shotwell caustically. "Not at all. I'm just ramming around through the dark making love to the squinch-owl. Come alive, you tub of lard. Are you damned shore you didn't hear or see anybody ride in here besides us?"

Bones began to bristle. "I said so, didn't I," he snapped. "And just because you're sheriff, Brood Shotwell, is no sign you can go around calling folks names, regardless. Maybe I am kinda plump, but I can kick your teeth out if I get mad enough. Go easy on that tub of lard stuff."

"There's a horse down at the corrals — Bill Morgan's big sorrel," said Shotwell coldly. "That bronc was stolen off the street of Twin Buttes by Buck Comstock. Now it is out here. You're plumb shore that Comstock didn't ride that bronc in here?"

Bones stared at the sheriff in amazement. "You must be loco! I hear this afternoon that Buck Comstock had been sentenced to twenty-five years in Pinole by

45

that weak minded old fool of a Judge Henning. I hear that you had Buck locked up tight in yore calaboose in town — and that you were going to start tomorrow for Pinole with him. Now you try and tell me he stole Bill's sorrel and rode it out to this ranch. What kind of a joke is this?"

"Joke be damned!" spat Shotwell. "Comstock made a getaway tonight and rode that sorrel out of town. The bronc is here. Comstock must have rode it in."

Bones seemed to be trying mightily to get all this news straight in his round, close clipped head. He opened his mouth and closed it two or three times, gulped — then shrugged. "This whole thing shore is news to me," he asserted stoutly. "If Buck Comstock rode that sorrel into this ranch, he shore must have come in awful quiet. I never heard nothin' — I never saw nothin'. I didn't even know that bronc was here. I tell you, I ain't seen hide or hair of a soul coming into this ranch since Dave Wagg rode in just before supper time and told me and the boys that Buck had been cinched for twenty-five years. That's all I can tell you, except this. If old Buck did make a getaway, I shore hope you break both legs and your back before you catch him again. Now you can chaw on that or

46

leave it alone, if the chawin' hurts your teeth."

Brood Shotwell cursed savagely, furiously — stamping back and forth. "You so-called good citizens!" he raved. "You yelp for law and order. You elect a man sheriff of your damned county. You expect him to keep a flock of itchy trigger hombres in line — expect him to protect your property and calloused hides. Yet, when some jasper goes outside the law, thieving or killing — like Buck Comstock for example — if that jasper happens to be a friend of yours — you all go blind and deaf and string-haltered in the head. You ain't a bit of help to your sheriff — none whatever. Who's a bigger fool than the man who tries to be a sheriff for a bunch of contrary galoots like you hairpins?"

"Heh — heh!" wheezed Bones. "I'll bite, Brood. Who?"

Shotwell went into another fury of cursing. A cowboy came running up through the dark. "Say Brood," he panted, "did you notice close how the reins of that sorrel bronc are tied? That bronc ain't been dragging those reins. They're looped over the horn."

"What of it?" snapped Shotwell. "That don't mean anything."

"I wonder," shrugged the cowboy. "It could mean that somewhere between here and town Comstock got off that bronc, turned it loose and dodged out on foot. He'd know that the sorrel, left alone and with reins tied up, would come straight home to this ranch. He'd know that we'd follow the sorrel's trail, and that we'd ride right past him."

"So what?" grunted Shotwell sourly. "What good would that have done him?"

"Well, he could have cut north into that malpais country around the buttes. And then again, maybe he circled back on foot for town where he could pick up another bronc and shag it the other direction. Buck Comstock's got it in him to be a mighty foxy hombre, if you ask me."

The idea sobered Shotwell for a moment. Then he shook his head slowly. "Not likely. Comstock was raised in the saddle. He wouldn't give up a perfectly good horse to do his traveling on foot — least of all when he'd know I'd be after him."

Bill Morgan spoke, in his deep, rolling tones. "In this case he might. It would be just like Buck, knowing that the sorrel was my pet bronc, to use it only as long as he absolutely had to and then turn it loose to come home. Though the darned chump

48

ought to know that I'd give him that sorrel or any other bronc — or all the broncs I own, if they'd help him get away."

Shotwell whirled on Bill, scowling. "That kind of talk —."

"Listen, Brood," cut in Morgan. "I've never been a hypocrite. If I'm against a man, I'm against him. If I'm for him — I'm for him, and the whole damn world is welcome to the news. Right now I'm for Buck Comstock — all the way, and I don't give a tinker's damn who knows it. Buck's my good friend. He got a dirty, rotten deal in that monkey trick trial this afternoon. I told that to Judge Henning, right in his teeth. I'm telling the same to you, now. Yeah — Buck Comstock is my friend, and I hope he gets away — clean. I hope you founder yourself trying to catch up with him. And if I thought that by blowing your head off, right here where you stand, it would make Buck dead shore to get away, I'd be more than likely to drag a gun and chance it. I reckon that makes it plain where my sympathies are."

Shotwell cursed again and whirled toward his horse. "We're going back and take a look at that malpais country," he yelled to his posse. "Come on. We're riding."

In a surge and creak of saddle gear they

were gone, back the way they had come. But Bill Morgan remained with Bones, who was looking out into the night with a twinkle of satisfaction in his eyes. Morgan, however, was moody and scowling and worried.

"Why did that darned chump of a Buck turn that sorrel loose to come home?" he growled. "He could have kept the bronc and welcome. Me, I got a good idea to throw a saddle on a spare bronc, take the sorrel and cut around into that malpais ahead of Shotwell and his posse and see if I can locate Buck and put him in a saddle again. If he's up there afoot, he won't have a Chinaman's chance."

"Don't you worry none about ole Buck," murmured Bones softly. "He's been took care of — already."

Morgan whirled, fixed alert, eager eyes on his cook. "Then you mean — ?"

"Yup," nodded Bones. "Buck was here. He rode the sorrel in. I give him some grub and blankets and guns. He took that grullo Indian pony and that old Yuma saddle which Slim Devine left here and never sent for when he went up to the Dakotas. And Buck, he's to hell and gone over on Cotton Valley by this time."

Bill Morgan thumped Bones in his fat

stomach. "Come inside while I kiss you, you fat old fox," exulted the cattleman. "Come inside and tell me all about it."

In the seclusion of the cook's room, Bones told his story, while Morgan listened eagerly. "So Buck hightailed it out on the grullo," Bones ended. "And the last thing he told me was this. You're to meet him at Indian Spring around midnight tomorrow. He said he wanted to have a big powwow with you. And he said for us to clam up and not mention a word to anybody else. Buck seemed plumb excited and eager about it, Bill, like as though he'd stumbled across a gold mine, or something. There you have it."

"Indian Spring," muttered Bill Morgan. "I'll be there. You bet. Bones, I think I'll give you a raise in wages."

"You will like hell," snorted Bones. "I didn't help Buck out for pay. I did it because I like him, because he's my good friend. And I did it because I don't think he was any more guilty of murder than you or me, Bill. Why when Dave Wagg told me that orry-eyed old pelican of a Judge Henning had give Buck twenty-five years in Pinole I like to broke down and blubbered like a kid. I couldn't hardly swallow my evening grub I was so broke up. And when

51

I laid down and tried to read I could hardly get my thoughts straightened out. I couldn't even see the print more'n half the time. It shore got me, thinking of a high class boy like Buck Comstock, due to put in twenty-five years in that hell hole of a penitentiary. And was I glad when he showed up — free and ready to ride. Mama!"

"The whole trial was a farce, Bones," said Morgan. "If ever a man was railroaded — cold — that man was Buck Comstock. The jury was handpicked, with ten of the twelve J Bar C men — Jaeger and Cutts' riders. The other two were Toad Black and Duke Younger. You know the breed Black and Younger are. If two more worthless whelps ever came down the pike, I don't know when it was. Buck didn't have a chance. Leek Jaeger and Frank Cutts pulled the strings all the way."

"How about young Curt Wallace? He's a law shark. Couldn't he do anything for Buck?"

"Did all any man could. But I'm telling you, the whole thing was cooked and ready to serve. That old swivel eared cow crane of a Judge Henning — hell, he wouldn't give young Wallace a chance. Every time the kid would open his mouth to put up an argument in Buck's defense, Henning would light all over him and spur him with a lot of words that I never could figure out the meaning of. No, that kid lawyer never had a chance."

"You make it sound almost like Judge Henning was acting under orders," said Bones thoughtfully. "And Shotwell — Brood Shotwell —."

"I don't know exactly how to figure Shotwell. Brood is a funny jigger. He's a gruff, surly sort of a cuss, but always, up until this mess he's always been a pretty fair sort of a sheriff, far as I can see. Now — I dunno. Still and all, come to think of it, he didn't act any other way than he's supposed to. He didn't take sides — he didn't open his mouth. He testified of course, about going out after Ben Sloan's body. But the way he gave his testimony, he didn't throw anything for or against Buck. He just gave facts and let it go at that. If Brood is tangled up with that crowd, he shore played his cards mighty smooth and cunning. Right now I'm withholding judgment on Brood. I'll give him the benefit of the doubt, which is a hell of a lot more than that court gave Buck Comstock."

"Well," said Bones slowly — "I don't know anything about that. But I do know that I believe in law and order — providing it plays its card fair and unbiased. If Buck Comstock had really murdered Ben Sloan in cold blood — even though Buck had been a good friend of mine — I'd say take him and give him the works. But nobody could ever convince me that Buck would do such a thing. Buck would never have pulled a gun and cut Ben Sloan down if Sloan hadn't gone for his war stick first. Buck just ain't the sort to kill unless he's drove to it in self-defense. So it must have been self-defense when he rocked off Ben Sloan, and in my cattygorry of things, self-defense never was murder. I'd ride to hell chasin' that fact."

"I reckon that's saying about all there is to say," nodded Morgan. "Your feelings and mine line up plumb even in this matter, Bones. And so, feeling like we do, we'll stick to Buck, root hog or die."

After leaving the Circle Star, Buck Comstock rode the whole night out, heading directly east. This route took him into Cotton Valley. He did not go near his own little spread, the Half Moon. Buck was entirely too wise to make a mistake of that sort. For he knew that Brood Shotwell would be out to look the Half Moon over, hoping that the quarry would pull in there and thus leave a good trail to be followed. So, instead of going near the Half Moon, Buck cut straight across Cotton Valley a good three miles above his ranchhouse, using cattle trails as much as he could in the hopes that the cattle, moving back and forth along those trails, would soon cover the sign left by his grullo pony.

Once across Cotton Valley, Buck cut up over the long rim rock and drove out into the vast reaches of Big Sage Desert which lay beyond. Here was weird and desolate country, sparsely clothed with sage and juniper, skunk cabbage and creosote bush. At intervals flat shoulders of rock humped through, and Buck, wherever he could, traveled those patches of rock, blurring his trail and mixing it up as he went.

He took an almost boyish satisfaction in these maneuvers. Funny, how different he felt — how different the whole world looked to him. Back there in jail he had been depressed, hopeless, stoically resigned. But now he was exultant and tingling with life. This Big Sage Desert, for instance. Always before, when the business of cattle ranching had at times made it necessary to ride some of this desert, he'd damned the wilderness of sage and distance heartily, cussing the heat and the sand, and the barren hunger and thirst of it all.

But this night Big Sage was a beautiful place to Buck. In its vastness lay security. He knew from past experience when he'd gone out after strays, how tough it was to find them in Big Sage. And straying cattle made no pretense at hiding their trail. Therefore, with he himself using every advantage and subterfuge he could think up to blot his trail, he knew that Brood Shotwell would have his hands full ever trying to run down that trail.

Of course, Buck had heard it said that Spike St. Ives could read and ferret out signs like nobody's business. Buck told himself, with a little gust of savagery, that if Spike St. Ives came out along this trail alone, the desert might have a secret to hide. Buck had had little use for St. Ives before his arrest and trial. Now he had none at all. St. Ives might pack a deputy's star, but from now on, as far as Buck was concerned, that star would never cover up the fact that St. Ives was a damned heartless, blood hungry wolf of a man.

Sunrise found Buck a long way out on Big Sage. Buck soon realized that he'd made a mistake in not getting a couple of canteens at the Circle Star. He could have had them, just as well as not, but in the excitement and tenseness of the moment he'd forgotten them. It looked like a long thirsty day ahead for himself and the grullo.

Of course he could have cut south to the Sour Water breaks and found water, or he could have gone north to Indian Spring. But Buck had good reasons for not going to either place, just yet. A moving object was easy to pick up, out in comparatively flat country like Big Sage. And if Shotwell had managed to work the trail out as far as the edge of the desert, Buck was going to take no chances on being seen as he rode to Sour Water breaks.

As far as Indian Spring was concerned, he wouldn't ride that way either, for two reasons. One was the same reason he would not ride for Sour Water, the other because he had arranged a meeting with Bill Morgan at Indian Spring and he wanted to play absolutely safe in keeping all others unaware of the rendezvous. He owed that to good old Bill. He couldn't run any chance of having Bill get in wrong, though he knew in his heart that Bill Morgan would defy the lightning to aid a friend.

Buck found a shoulder of rock which jutted high enough to throw a pocket of shade, shade which would last until around midday. He dismounted, unsaddled the grullo, let it have a good roll in the sand, then brought it close in under the rock and tied it there. He spread the saddle blanket, ate a cold breakfast and had a smoke. Then, a final survey from the top of the rock which showed nothing but miles of endless sage and sand, already a dancing mirage under the heat of the sun, though the sun was hardly half an hour high. Yeah, it would be a long day, a hot and thirsty one. Buck didn't really mind. For he was free and in a position to fight.

He dropped down, stretched out in the shadow of the rock and slept. Along toward noon the sun reached him and woke him up. He endured the next few hours of baking heat stoically, tried to forget the thirst that flogged him savagely. Finally, the sun arced slowly over a thread of shade formed on the east side of the rock, and this both Buck and the grullo hugged eagerly.

Buck dozed again until sunset. Then he saddled up, and through the coiling blue shadows which flooded the desert, rode north.

CHAPTER THREE

It was about mid-afternoon when Bill Morgan cinched his silver mounted hull on the big sorrel, slung a canteen to the horn, stuffed a couple of sandwiches into his slicker roll and rode leisurely south through the center of Coyote Valley, stopping for a time at both the Rafter T and the Lazy F, where he held short confabs with the respective owners, Bud Tharp and Johnny Frazier. What he told these two good men left them whistling with musing smiles on their bronzed faces. Still traveling south, just at sundown, Morgan pulled in at the Stirrup Cross. There he ran into a distinct surprise. Old man Addis stood in front of the ranchhouse, engaged in heavy argument with none other than Leek Jaeger and Frank Cutts.

Bill Morgan's eyes narrowed slightly, then became bland and innocent as he drew up beside them, leaned over and rested his forearms across his saddle horn in a lazy slouch. He nodded. "Howdy, gents."

Old man Addis looked flustered. He was a narrow faced old fox, with thinning, sandy hair, a ragged, tired looking mustache, and pale eyes under bleached brows. Frank Cutts showed no change of expression on his coldly set features, but Leek Jaeger scowled openly at Morgan's arrival.

"Kind of a long way off your range, ain't you, Morgan?" growled Jaeger.

Morgan shrugged. "Not near as far off mine as you are off yours, Jaeger. Likewise and besides, as I see it, it's none of your damn business. By the way, what happened to your phiz? You look like a mule had kicked you."

Jaeger, his blocky face swollen and bruise blackened from the terrific blow Buck Comstock had hit him the night before, cursed savagely. "Shotwell was telling me this morning that you made some pretty long talk last night," he accused.

Bill Morgan lifted his eyebrows. "Oh, yeah. Suppose you talk a little straighter. That forked tongue of yours has a habit of going off slaunch-wise. Don't be mealy mouthed, Jaeger. If you got anything to say, spit it out."

"You told Shotwell that you hoped Comstock would get away," bawled Jaeger. "And you said that you'd help him any way you could."

"Correct," rumbled Morgan. "I said that. I meant it, too. Buck Comstock is my friend. I think a lot of him. I don't give two whoops and a holler who knows it. That takes in Shotwell, you and Cutts, that old hypocrite Henning and everybody else who's interested from here to the gates of purgatory. So what?"

"He's a fugitive from Law — a killer — a murderer," Jaeger spat.

"Part of that is true, most of it a damned lie," rasped Bill Morgan coldly. "He's a fugitive from law, damned cheap law, I might add. But he's no killer and no murderer. Any man who says he is, is a liar."

"I say he is," yelled the enraged Jaeger.

"Then the shoe fits you perfect," drawled Morgan, coldly watchful. "You're a liar, Jaeger."

Jaeger's swollen face twisted into a snarl, his right hand began to creep toward the gun at his hip. Morgan shifted slightly in the saddle. "I wouldn't, was I you, Jaeger," he said, his rumbling voice toning down to a cold, bell-like note. "You never saw the day when you could shade me. Here's an earful I want you to get. I never was much

61

for mealy mouthed hombres of your sort. I've lived my life among men who looked straight and talked straight and who, if they figgered they had a right to another man's scalp, went out and tried to take it — open and above board. But they never went sneaking behind a crooked court and crooked law. I was raised among men who did their own chores like men, right or wrong. I got to move along the way I was trained. The way I see it if a man's a liar, he's a liar, no matter how many big words he uses. If he's a crook, the same thing applies. You're both, Jaeger — in plain one syllable words. And get this right. You try and tangle any of your bought and sold law around me and I'll look you up and blow you down. The same takes in that chisel faced partner of yours. And if you think I'm not man enough to do the job, you got my permission to try and demonstrate — now!"

Old man Addis, his pale eyes flickering with a sudden fear, started to back away. Jaeger was licking his swollen lips, convulsed with a body shaking rage. Frank Cutts, his pale face expressionless, caught Jaeger by the arm and swung him partially around.

"Don't be a damned fool, Leek," he

rasped. "In the first place, you're acting like a kid. In the second you wouldn't have a ghost of a chance. Trading words like this doesn't mean a damned thing. Come on — you and I are all done here. We're riding."

Bill Morgan, smiling with his lips, but cold as ice about the eyes, watched the two men climb into their saddles and spur away. Then he looked at old man Addis. "What did those two jaspers have on their minds, Tom?" he drawled.

"Business — just a little business," answered Addis, testily. "Damn it all, Morgan — you don't realize how heavy worded you can be some times. You had no call to give the lie to Leek."

"I told Jaeger that any man who said Buck Comstock was a killer and a murderer, was a liar. I'm sticking to those words."

"Comstock put Ben Sloan in his grave, didn't he?" twanged Addis angrily. "If that don't make him a killer, I don't know what does."

"Wrong, Tom," said Morgan quietly. "A killer is a professional, a man who sells his guns — who works to get the edge before rolling smoke, who goes out with deliberate intent to cut a man down. But a man who throws a gun in self-defense, is no killer."

"The jury decided it wasn't a case of self-defense," Addis argued. "They decided that Comstock went out deliberately to get Ben Sloan — and got him. Comstock had a trial by law, Morgan — and was found guilty. That's good enough for me."

"That jury!" snorted Morgan with vast contempt. "They didn't sit on that box to give Buck Comstock a square deal. They were hand picked for just one purpose — to find Buck guilty. They never paid a damn bit of attention to the evidence. As far as they were concerned they could have given their verdict before that old squinch owl of a Judge Henning ever called for the first witness. Hell amilin', man — I was there, every day — every minute of that trial, and I know what I saw and heard. That jury! Don't quote 'em to me."

Old man Addis threw his hands up. "I ain't got time to stand here arguing all that over again. You got your opinion and I got mine. What brought you down this far, anyhow?"

"I had started out with the idea of business," Morgan said crisply. "But I've sorta changed my mind. I don't like the company I found you in, Tom. Nor the way you grab for the viewpoint of a couple of hombres like Jaeger and Cutts — who you've known only a few years in comparison to what amounts to almost a lifetime of acquaintance with me — and Buck Comstock. In my book, you just don't rate up any more, Tom. Sorry. Adios."

With that Morgan swung the sorrel and started back the way he had come. Old man Addis stared after him, narrow face twisted with a variety of conflicting emotions, of which anger was uppermost. Then Addis turned and stamped off to the corrals.

Dusk found Bill Morgan half way between the Stirrup Cross and the Lazy F. He had been watching his back trail carefully and now, finding it empty, seized upon the first deep blanket of shadows and turned the sorrel directly east. The budding stars found him crossing Cotton Valley, to leave that and then push up past the long rimrock and out onto the vast reaches of Big Sage Desert beyond. Here he turned the sorrel slightly northeast and set the animal to a steady jog.

Lacking perhaps fifteen minutes of midnight, Bill Morgan rode up to a dark bulk of jagged rock outcropping, sparsely fringed with sage and creosote bush. The night was illimitable, vast and silent. For a moment Morgan knew a qualm of worry. Perhaps, somewhere along the line, Buck Comstock might have run into trouble. Then a cool voice spoke out of the darkness. "Evening, Bill."

"Buck!" Morgan stepped from the saddle as Buck Comstock, a tall, lean shadow, moved up to him. They shook hands wordlessly. Then Morgan spoke gruffly. "You long legged whelp, you beat Johnny and Bud and me to it. You knew we were aiming to bust that cussed jail wide open and haul you out by the scruff of the neck. But you went and took a hell of a risk and made it by yourself. I saw Jaeger today. His face still looks like it had been sideswiped by a freight train. You shore must have poured it on with that punch. How you been making it, kid?"

"Fair enough. Put in kind of a thirsty day. Along with all the other stuff Bones gave me, I forgot a canteen. Me and the bronc darn near emptied this spring when we first hit it, but I'm feeling ready for a smoke about now. Which reminds me — tobacco was something else I forgot to ask

Bones for. I'm going to rob you of all you got, Bill."

"Your luck still holds," Morgan chuckled. "I always pack half a dozen extra sacks in my saddle-bags. Here, I'll get it for you."

They twirled smokes, squatted on their heels. The grullo, lonely for its kind, came shuffling out of the dark and stood contentedly beside the sorrel. A light wind, almost bitter with the redolence of sage in its breath, stirred about them. The pale light of the stars stretched strange and distorted shadows past man and horse.

"Bones said you had something you wanted to tell me, Buck," prompted Morgan.

Buck inhaled deeply, nodding. "I got a spark of an idea, just before I made that jail break. In fact, it was that idea, as much as anything else which made me take the chance on Shotwell's guns. I've done a lot of thinking since then and the more I think and play with that idea the more I seem to see. It's kinda like a puzzle with one part missing. Long as you haven't got that key part, you can't make heads or tails of your puzzle. Then, when you get hold of that key part, the whole thing is plain and easy to solve. Maybe, Bill — you've been wondering how Jaeger happened to be present in the jail when I made my getaway."

Morgan nodded. "That's right, I have."

"Well, here's something that'll make you prick up your ears plenty. Jaeger came in with Shotwell to lay a proposition in front of me. He said that if I'd sign over my Cotton Valley range to him, he'd see that my sentence was cut from twenty-five to five years. What do you make of that?"

Morgan let out an explosive breath. "It just proves that I was right when I called Judge Henning a weasel faced old crook — when I said that the jury was packed and that you'd been railroaded. It also suggests that somewhere in the dirty scheme behind it all there's some weak spots which Jaeger is afraid might pop up and raise hell."

"Exactly," nodded Buck. "It proves that and suggests a lot else. Like I said, I been doing a lot of thinking since last night, Bill. Here, look at this."

Buck drew three parallel furrows on the starlit sand. "Figure this to be Twin Buttes range. We got three valleys, Timber Valley, Coyote Valley and Cotton Valley all laying side by side. The middle valley, Coyote — is the richest of the three. Best water, best grass, best shelter. Leek Jaeger and Frank Cutts started business on the J Bar C, which they got from Bob Hafey. Some folks say they bought that spread, fair and upright. Others claim it was euchered from Bob Hafey over the poker table Cutts used to run in the Belle Union saloon. Anyway, that's neither here nor there. The main fact is — they got it. In no time at all they got control of all of Timber Valley. I don't pretend to know how they got that either — yet they got it.

"Now then, with my own ears I one time heard that cattle buyer, Ed Fitch, tell Leek Jaeger that if the J Bar C didn't quit stocking Timber Valley range so heavy, they'd strip it. Jaeger laughed and made the crack that there was a lot of other range around Twin Buttes that he and Cutts intended to control before they were done. What other range is there, except Coyote and Cotton Valleys?"

"None," grunted Morgan — "leastways, none that's worth a damn. Go on — go on. You interest me, boy — you interest me."

"Fair enough. Time was when Ben Sloan and I got along well enough. We never were exactly bosom chums, but we were able to pass each other by without taking on a spell of indigestion. Then Sloan started changing. He began to show pretty mean and sulky, but I didn't bother none about it, figuring he'd outgrow anything that was twisting him. He didn't outgrow it — he got worse. Finally, one day in town he accused me of sleepering some of his stuff. I laughed at him and told him he was crazy. He got so he wouldn't even talk to me. Then came that day — well, you know what happened, Bill. He accused me again of tampering with his stock, and I got mad. You might laugh off being called a cow thief the first time. But the second time it begins to get under your skin. Yeah, I got mad. I told Sloan he was a liar. He went for his gun, came ashootin'. It was him or me. I got him.

"Now, Ben Sloan is dead — and I'm dodging the law. There isn't a thing to keep the J Bar C from moving into Cotton Valley. If Jaeger had bluffed me into signing over my Cotton Valley holdings it would have been a big help — made it easier for the J Bar C to move in. Let's suppose the J Bar C moves into Cotton Valley. Where does that leave the Coyote Valley range?"

"Right in the middle of the J Bar C holdings and shore as hell to be swallowed up, sooner or later," rapped out Morgan tersely. "Buck, old timer — you've made a picture — you've made a picture."

70

Buck inhaled deeply. "It shore looks that way to me, Bill."

"Clever," rumbled Morgan — "clever as hell. Ben Sloan always did have an ugly temper. By setting him against you it was a cinch that he'd force gunplay, sooner or later. No question but what Jaeger and Cutts had some of their men sleeper some Wineglass critters to make it look like your work. They wanted to get Sloan to make the break. They could have figured that it wouldn't have mattered a tinker's damn one way or the other, as long as either you or Sloan got killed. Then they'd have the other fellow up for murder and railroad him. That would leave Cotton Valley wide open. And if they could have bluffed the survivor into the kind of deal Jaeger wanted of you, that would have set them up more than pretty. And Jaeger is smart enough to know that if you had accepted the deal it would have been, in the eyes of most folks, an admission of guilt, Buck. Then, when the J Bar C moved on to your range, folks wouldn't have thought anything about it. On the other hand, if the J Bar C set out to gobble your range too quick after the trial, a lot of ears would have been open to the railroading talk that me and Bud and Johnny have been making. Oh, I get it now — I get the whole dirty, smooth coyote idea."

"Thought you would, Bill," nodded Buck. "It's just like that puzzle I was telling you about — easy enough to figure out, once you get the key idea."

"And the answer, Buck — is what?"

"The answer is — that the J Bar C doesn't get a foothold in Cotton Valley," said Buck with fierce grimness. "There never was anything more true than the old saying about an ounce of prevention, Bill. The chore of keeping them out is going to be tough, but not half as tough as running them out if they should once get a foothold. Once they dig in there, Bill — you and Bud and Johnny can begin counting the days until your finish. For it isn't Cotton Valley they're really after. It's Coyote Valley they want."

"Correct. You got any plan to suggest?"

"Yeah. My range is still my range, even though I am on the dodge from Brood Shotwell just now. But the Wineglass, Ben Sloan's old spread — well, if Jaeger and Cutts can get hold of that, they got their foothold. Your play, Bill — as I see it, is to beat 'em to the Wineglass. If Sloan ever had any kin, I never heard about it. But the chances are, he has, somewhere. What you should do is line it for town, first thing to-morrow, get hold of Curt Wallace and tell him to get busy trying to run down a line on the nearest kin of Ben Sloan. When and if he does locate them, you offer to buy the Wineglass. Between you and Johnny and Bud, you should be able to swing the deal. And if Jaeger and Cutts try and move in, call 'em — call 'em cold. Make them show their authority for taking over the Wine-glass — for just as shore as you and me are sitting here, they're going to try and grab the Wineglass off."

"Correct again, Buck," Morgan nodded. "One hundred per cent correct. I'll do it. I'll have Curt Wallace on the job first thing in the morning. I know Bud and Johnny will see the right of this. They'll back our hand, all the way. Kid, you've done a lot of mighty clear and straight thinking to get this thing figured out."

Buck laughed grimly. "I don't know any-thing about that, Bill. But I do know that it hit me pretty clear that Jaeger wouldn't have made that proposition to me just to get my range. He hates me too bad. I knew right away he was after a lot bigger game than my little Half Moon spread. And when I set to figuring out just what it was he was really after, there was only one answer that fitted. From then on the whole picture was clear."

Morgan stood up. "I'll be drifting. You got me all spurred up and anxious to run. I'll be waiting at Curt Wallace's door when he gets out of bed. You making out all right? Got plenty of grub?"

"Shore. I can take care of myself, now. I always was more or less of a night hawk. I'll probably drop in at the Circle Star some night and see you. I'm going to be anxious to hear how things are progressing."

"You take it easy," warned Morgan. "No long chances, remember. Brood Shotwell — you know what a bloodhound he can be. He'll stick after you until hell freezes. He's been more'n savage about the way you fooled him."

Buck laughed softly. "He'll have to ride faster and further and jump quicker than he ever did before in his life if he wants to get me again. By the way, Bill — if a bronc or two of yours turn up missing every now and then, don't get excited. You'll know who is riding them."

"Help yourself, kid," Morgan chuckled. "I'll pass that same word to Johnny and Bud. Maybe it might be handier to pick up one of theirs every so often. So — watch

yourself, don't take any fool chances —
and trust me to get plumb immediate action, in more ways than one. So long."

They shook hands again and Morgan
was soon lost in the night. Buck, whistling
softly between his teeth, resaddled his
grullo, swung astride and lifted the reins.
When he turned in again to get a couple of
hours of sleep, he was a good ten miles
from Indian Spring.

In the chill greyness of the desert dawn,
Buck cooked and ate a meager breakfast,
saddled the grullo and struck out, riding a
wide and watchful circle. He was not going
to make the mistake of underestimating
the resourceful stubbornness of Brood
Shotwell. Shotwell was a born man-hunter
and had grown old and grizzled at the
game. There were few tricks of the trade
which the sheriff did not know. He was a
fox who would bear watching.

Yet, even with the knowledge that Shotwell would be riding and looking and
watching all the time, Buck was cheerful.
Back there in the Twin Buttes jail, before
the great light had burst upon him, Buck
had been, as he had admitted to himself
more than once, plenty low in mind and
spirits. Somehow then it had seemed that
he was so hemmed in with the withes and

tithes of law, he didn't have a ghost of a show, not a chance. And he had reached a point where he almost didn't give a damn any more — the point of being fatalistic. His mind had seemed numb, his perceptions blunted. He had already been about to accept a prison philosophy of what was the use. Everything was set against him, there wasn't a loophole and everything was hopeless.

But then, as his mind grasped the significance of Jaeger's scheme, he had galvanized to a new courage, a new determination. He had glimpsed a weak spot in Jaeger's armor and was going to take a cut at it. He had made a long and dangerous gamble in his getaway, but it was a gamble that had won. Now he was riding the free open world once more and he had, through good old Bill Morgan, set machinery in motion which Jaeger and Cutts would find mighty hard to stop. Also, gleaming far out in the future somewhere, still a little indistinct and uncertain, perhaps — but there nevertheless, was a star of hope for his own future. For it was not at all unlikely now that when the J Bar C had its hand called, as it most certainly would be, facts would come to light which would exonerate him and open the Avenue of Life full and wide once more. It was a good thought to hang on to and not at all difficult when you were only twenty-six and the good red tide of blood ran strong in your veins and you wanted to go on and drink the cup of the future to the full.

So it was, reasoning thus, Buck whistled cheerfully as he rode, welcoming the rays of the morning sun, and finding a strange and exhilarating satisfaction in watching the sage wrens flit here and there, and an occasional long eared jack rabbit scud fleetly away. Freedom! A wonderful, precious thing. Without freedom there could never be any real point to living, no joy in existence.

Noon found Buck some half dozen miles north of the Wineglass headquarters and at mid-afternoon he was less than two hundred yards from the ranch buildings, flattened out on his stomach in a patch of thigh deep wild oats which fringed the top of a low ridge. In the gully in back of the ridge, the grullo Indian pony stood ground reined, rolling its bit ring busily as it grazed.

Buck could hardly have told why he had come to this place. It wasn't the safest thing to do by any means. The far reaches of the Big Sage Desert were a much more secure sanctuary for a man who had Sheriff Brood Shotwell on his trail. But Buck was too young, too restless, too eager to be somewhere near this new fight that was going to be waged. His own interests were at stake, his own future. He couldn't go on skulking around in Big Sage waiting and wondering and stewing. He had to know! And so, there he was, peering cautiously through the tawny wild oats, watching the ranch buildings below. This, he was sure, would be the battleground for control of Cotton Valley. It was more accessible for the J Bar C than was his own ranch, farther south. Here was where Jaeger and Cutts would try and sink their greedy claws.

Except for a single horse, standing ground reined in the shade of a feed shed, the Wineglass headquarters seemed deserted. Just where the rider of that horse was, Buck did not know — nor could he figure out who it could be. Ben Sloan had kept only two regular riders, picking up two or three extra hands during roundup and branding and then laying them off again when the rush was over with. These two regulars had been Ace Parker and Curly Jenkins. Perhaps that bronc down there belonged to one of those two.

Buck soon found out differently. A hulking, bulky shouldered figure left the ranchhouse and sauntered over to the ground reined bronco. He took something out of the saddlebags, then started back toward the ranchhouse once more. Buck Comstock stiffened and a growl of fury rose in his throat. He knew that hulking figure down there. All through the long, depressing hours of the trial, that man had been one of the twelve Buck had watched and wondered at. That fellow was Toad Black, one of the jury — the jury that had adjudged Buck guilty of murder.

Buck had brought his Winchester up to the ridge top with him. Now he caught up the weapon, half raised it. The impulse was on him savagely to draw down on Toad Black and knock him kicking. Then he got a grip on himself, lowered the gun. He wasn't a bushwhacker, no matter how much he hated — no matter how much a polecat like Toad Black deserved killing. And this whole play called for headwork, just now. Violence would no doubt come along later. But just now smart thinking was worth more.

What was Toad Black doing out here at the Wineglass? He had never at any time, as far as Buck knew, worked for Ben Sloan.

Yet he was here now, hanging around, killing time. Maybe he had been sent out to guard the place. Maybe Leek Jaeger had sent him out.

While Buck was wondering about this, Toad Black came to a halt beside the ranchhouse and built a cigarette. Buck, watching him, realized suddenly that Black was staring intently out toward the west. The man saw something which had startled and interested him. Abruptly Black whirled and ducked swiftly into the ranchhouse.

Buck's glance immediately followed that look Black had thrown. Out there, coming straight for the ranch buildings, still some four or five hundred yards distant, was a rider on a liver and white pinto bronc. A slim rider wearing a white shirt and a new white Stetson hat. Even as Buck frowned his wonderment, the pinto dipped into a little hollow and out of sight.

When the pinto next appeared, considerably closer, Buck got a new start of surprise. That rider was a woman. No mistake about it. A woman, all right. And a strange one. Women were not very plentiful on the Twin Buttes range, and of those who were there, none that Buck knew, and he knew them all, wore riding breeches, high, glossy

Cordovan riding boots and a white silk blouse. But this woman did. By the sheen of the material, even at this distance, Buck knew that white blouse was of silk.

Buck was all eyes. Whoever she was, she sure made a nice picture as she swung easily and lithely to the jog of the pinto bronc. She had a good seat in a saddle, one of poised, straight backed grace. The pinto was making easy work of it, carrying a slim, light rider like that. She was turning her head from side to side, no doubt enjoying the sunlight and the wide vistas of sweeping, shimmering range. And it was not until she pulled to a halt before the ranchhouse and was about to dismount, did Buck remember Toad Black!

Buck lunged almost upright, but ingrained caution dropped him flat again. This was no business of his. Maybe she had arranged to meet Toad Black here at the deserted Wineglass headquarters. Buck knew immediately that he was wrong in this surmise. For one thing, if such a meeting had been arranged, Toad Black would not have dodged so precipitately from sight when he first glimpsed her approach. For another, what woman, least of all a woman like this one, would ever have anything to do with Toad Black — who wasn't called Toad for nothing. A big, black browed, lowering brute of a man, with a flat face and horrible bulbous eyes. . . .

The girl walked into the house, moving with the same smooth grace she had shown in the saddle. She had taken off her hat and was swinging it in her hand. Buck saw that her hair was very dark and that the sun shone on it so brilliantly as to give the effect of a sort of halo about her head. In two more strides she was out of sight.

Buck stared at the ranchhouse intently, frowning and savage. He was of half a mind to throw caution to the wind and go on down there. More than once he'd heard stories concerning Toad Black's methods with women. Maybe —.

This time Buck did lunge clear to his feet. For, carrying up the slope to him came the thin, high panic of a woman's scream — and there was utter terror in the sound!

A reckless curse broke from Buck's lips and the next instant he was racing down the slope toward the ranchhouse.

CHAPTER FOUR

Bill Morgan rode into Twin Buttes through the first slanting rays of the rising sun. Long miles and a sleepless night had etched lines of gauntness about the old cattleman's grim, leathery face, but his eyes, though deep sunken from fatigue, were bright and cold and purposeful.

As Morgan pulled up in front of the hotel, two men came jingling along from the livery barn, Brood Shotwell and his deputy, Spike St. Ives. Both looked harsh and savage and weary, like they had just come from spending many long and fruit-less hours in the saddle. Morgan smiled grimly to himself.

"Mornin', Brood," he drawled.

The sheriff grunted and made as if to pass, then swung back to face Morgan. "Oh, I get it," growled Shotwell. "I can read the look in your eye. No — Spike and me didn't locate any trail worth while — but we will, Morgan — count on that, we will. Unless Comstock has cleared plumb out of this range, we'll get him, sooner or later. And while I'm about it, I got a little question to ask you. Where were you, all last night?"

"Who said I was anywhere?" countered Morgan.

"You went all the way south to the Stirrup Cross late yesterday afternoon. Then you kind of drifted out of sight and just about made a night of it somewhere. You weren't at the Circle Star about eleven o'clock last night. I know, because Spike and I came by that way."

Morgan rolled a cigarette. "Have I rustled any cattle?" he drawled. "Have I stole any horses? Have I killed anybody? In other words, have I done a single damn thing that makes it any of your business where I was or what I was doing?"

"You could have been out somewhere meeting Comstock," rapped the sheriff. "I got a hunch you were. If I could prove it —."

"Ah!" chuckled Morgan. "If you could only prove so many things, Brood. But you can't. And even if you could prove that I'd been holding a little habla with Buck Comstock in Tom Addis' parlor, it wouldn't do you any good. You couldn't do anything about it."

"The hell I couldn't," snarled Shotwell. "I'd throw you behind bars to cool your heels for a while."

"Wrong, Brood — wrong. For one thing, you ain't got much of a jail left, after that fire the other night. For another, anytime you go to throw Bill Morgan in the jug you want to have plenty of cause — plenty. And you want to see me first and club me down with a whiffle-tree. Else I won't arrest worth a damn. Don't go wasting your breath on threats, Brood. You're not bullying a kid."

Spike St. Ives, silent up to now, cursed bitterly. "What a lot of you wise jaspers in these parts need is a gut-full of hot lead. You'd find out then just who is running this range."

Morgan looked at St. Ives in open contempt. "I know that now. I know who thinks he's running this range. Leek Jaeger. He thinks he is and so do you. That's why, when he barks you two brave representatives of the law lay down and roll over. Brood, here's an earful it might pay you to listen to. If you want the decent folks in these parts to respect the authority of your star, you show us something to respect about you, the man. Until you do show us that, don't squeal if you get laughed at."

With this terse broadside, Bill Morgan turned his back, climbed the hotel steps and went in. He went upstairs and along the hall to Curt Wallace's room, where he knocked. At a sleepy summons he entered and closed the door behind him. Curt was sitting on the edge of the bed, just pulling on his pants. He started up in alarm. "They didn't get — Buck — ?"

"No," rumbled Morgan, kicking up a chair. "They didn't get him and most likely won't. But I got something to tell you, Curt — that'll make your ears fan in the wind. Here it is."

Then Morgan told of his meeting with Buck and of all Buck had told him and of the deductions the two of them had arrived at concerning cause and effect. The final thing was the matter concerning the heir of Ben Sloan.

"Buck said he didn't know if Sloan even had kin of any sort, but he expected he must have, somewhere," ended Morgan. "Your job, Curt, is to rustle like hell and locate whichever of that kin the Wineglass range will go to. When you do, buy it, if the price is anywhere near reasonable. Buy it, even if the price ain't reasonable. Bud Tharp and Johnny Frazier and I will pool our rolls to get it.

By one hook or crook we got to get that ranch. So you get busy, right away. You can draw on me for any immediate expense money you need."

Curt Wallace had stood up, was staring at Morgan. "Good Lord, Bill — do you mean to tell me you didn't know?"

"Know? Know what?"

"That Jean Harper is Ben Sloan's heir?"

"Who the devil is Jean Harper?" blurted the startled Morgan.

"Miss Jean Harper. She's the girl who was with Jaeger and Cutts in the courtroom the last day of the trial. She's staying out at the J Bar C ranch."

Bill Morgan gulped, seemed lost for a moment. "That means —."

"Exactly," nodded Curt Wallace grimly. "It means that Buck figured out the moves Jaeger and Cutts intend to take, right to an eyelash. But it means that Jaeger and Cutts have beaten your time, Bill. They got Ben Sloan's heir right out at their ranch and you can see what chance we got to get hold of the Wineglass, now."

Bill Morgan was too much of a fighter to stay down very long. His jaw jutted, his eyes flashed. "Don't give a damn if they have got the girl out at the J Bar C," he rasped. "That's no sign that she's sold to them — or even intends to sell. You bust right in out there and have a talk with her. We're going to fight this thing through to the last damn lick. Get busy!"

Buck Comstock was within less than a hundred yards of the Wineglass ranch-house when a thought struck him that sent a trickle of ice up his backbone, turned his mouth to a parched and leathery dryness. Maybe the whole set-up was a trap. Maybe he had not been as unobserved as he thought. Maybe there were other men in that ranchhouse besides Toad Black, men looking at him over gun sights this very moment. Maybe within the next stride or two a blast of venomous lead would rip his life out.

Buck's brain seemed almost numb as all of these possibilities struck him, one after another. Yet, he realized, almost fatalistically, that if he had been suckered, if he had been tricked, there was nothing he could do about it now. He couldn't stop and go back. He was in the open, the wide open — there wasn't a shred of protection within yards and yards of him. It was farther back to the top of the ridge than it was to the ranchhouse. All he could do was gamble and believe that the scream he had heard was a genuine one, that the instinctive call to manhood and chivalry which had sent him racing headlong for the ranchhouse, had real basis for action. So, doggedly, he drove on.

Again sounded that forlorn, hopeless, terrified cry. And now Buck knew that he had not been tricked. There was no falsity, no pretense in that wail. The mortal fear in it was stark, heart-rending. Buck's eyes turned bleak and savage and muscles tautened all over him until he was a charging bulk of hard, relentless fury. He lunged for the door, but was still a stride or two distant, when a tangle of fighting figures spun from it, out into the white, searching sunlight.

She seemed incredibly frail in the pawing clutches of that hulking beast who was Toad Black. Already he had torn one sleeve of sheer silk completely off her blouse and the white soft curves of her arm were banded with red and dark purple where the clawing fingers of Toad Black had bruised her flesh. At this moment Black had her by both shoulders, trying to drag her close to him, while his horrible, protruding eyes and lecherous mouth mocked her. She was fighting gallantly, but hopelessly.

A feral, red haze swept across Buck Comstock's vision and through it he could see but one object — that face of Toad Black. Buck forgot he had guns at his hips, forgot everything but an insane, crazy, surging desire to kill and crush with his bare hands. He darted in close behind the struggling girl and looked past her into the startled eyes of Toad Black. The next moment Buck hit him, his fist traveling right over the top of the girl's dark head.

Buck put everything he had into that punch. He knew a wild joy as the shock of it ran up through clenched fist and taut wrist, through driving forearm and shoulder. He could feel his knuckles, like hurtling flint, pulp the flesh, split it open and bite up against the very bone. Toad Black had let go of the girl as he saw that punch start and threw both hands, ugly hairy paws they were, up in a futile effort to ward the blow off. He was much too slow. And now, under the lethal power of the punch he tottered backward, slammed against the wall of the ranchhouse, dropped to his knees and fell over on his side.

Buck swept the dazed girl to one side and lunged forward. Black wasn't out — he was clawing for the gun at his hip. Buck drove a shrewd, savage kick, which caught Black on the forearm and the renegade's gun flipped harmlessly through the air. Then, his hands clawing and reaching, Buck went for the fellow's throat.

Toad Black was far from through. In that big, hulking carcass of his lay a frightful reservoir of brute strength, and he managed to ward off Buck's reaching fingers, roll over with surprising speed and lunge to his feet.

Toad's face was a gory wreck from that first terrific punch. His froggy eyes seemed to protrude more than ever. His yellow teeth showed beneath his pulped and flattened nose in a simian-like snarl. With both huge arms clubbed and swinging, he rushed at Buck, who sidestepped and nearly tore Black's ear off with another rapier blow.

Black gave a weird, coughing bawl of fury as he spun and staggered wildly, again thrown off balance by the power of Buck's lashing fist. He was like nothing so much as a mad, wounded gorilla.

Buck slithered after him and caught him again as he was turning, and he laid Black's jaw wide open from temple to chin. Buck knew that he had never hit any man so hard in his life, yet, somehow, Black kept his feet. It was like hitting something inhuman.

Buck moved in, trying for a clear shot at the point of Black's jaw. And one of the renegade's wildly clubbing fists caught Buck on the side of the head. The white fire of agony bathed Buck from head to toe, his senses reeled and crazy lights blazed before his eyes. It was as if he had been hit by a post maul.

Instinct alone caused Buck to duck and it seemed as if he had been scalped as another whizzing fist skimmed across the top of his head. Then Black caught him and dragged him close. Only the utter fury which galvanized the renegade at the moment kept Buck from being broken and trampled like a reed. For Toad Black was a mad thing now. He tore and clawed at Buck like some berserk animal. He was mewing and snarling and snuffing like that same animal. Blood from his split and pulped face spouted all over Buck and the raw stench of it was sickening.

Strangely enough, this shaking and slamming around had the effect of clearing Buck's tortured head. And his own rage and fury flared up anew, particularly so when Black tried wickedly to knee him. Buck twisted his hips aside, dropped both fists and then sank them deep into Black's gross body.

Black gasped and Buck knew, with savage exultancy, that those blows had hurt Black, hurt him plenty. He pumped more punches into the same spot and Black, groaning and retching, gave ground. Buck swarmed after him, smashing him savagely in the body. Black stumbled back faster and faster, spreading both hairy paws across his middle in an effort to ward off that punishment which seemed to be tearing him in half.

Buck switched his attack suddenly, driving a ripping left into Black's face. The blow hurled the renegade against the side of the ranchhouse and as he seemed to bounce back, his sagging jaw loomed fair and open. Power rippled up Buck Comstock's lean body, rippled up from his very heels, arcing through straightening knees, narrow hips and wide, driving shoulders. At the end of that surge of power was Buck's right fist, finding the very point of Toad Black's jaw. The sound was as if a stout board had been split. Toad Black's feet crossed, he spun half around and went down with a crash. He lay like a dead man.

Buck staggered back. He almost went down himself. His knees were trembling, his feet clumsy and uncertain. Everything was dancing and whirling about him. He couldn't see very well, his eyes seemed full of blood. Those few mad moments of utter fury seemed to have drained every atom of strength from him. He reached out and leaned against the wall of the ranchhouse to keep from going down beside Black. He stood there, weaving and tottering, gulping hoarsely for air to feed his tortured lungs. For the moment he had forgotten all about the girl.

He passed a slow hand before his eyes, as though he would wipe away that crimson mist before them. He stared down at the crumpled bulk of Toad Black. A tough hombre, Black — an awful tough hombre.

Now Buck remembered the girl and he swung slowly around, rested the flat of his shoulders against the wall and stared at her. She stood off there a little way, looking first at Buck, then at Toad Black, then back at Buck again. She was crying soundlessly, tears rolling down her cheeks. Her lips opened and closed, as though she were trying to say something, though no words came. One hand was rubbing the other arm, where Black's brutal fingers had mauled and bruised her.

Buck shook himself, fought a lop-sided grin to his face. " 'S all right — now," he panted. "Everything — is all right. That — hog — won't come back for quite some time. But God — it was like hitting a stone wall. Don't cry, lady — you're safe enough — now."

Abruptly he realized that she was staring at him, her wide eyes shocked, almost unbelieving. "You," she quavered. "Y— you! You're — Buck Comstock — the man who — killed my uncle. The man who broke jail!"

Now Buck recognized her. This was the girl who had stood between Leek Jaeger and Frank Cutts and had recoiled at the sight of him as Brood Shotwell and Spike St. Ives had taken him from the courtroom after Judge Henning had sentenced him. This was that girl!

The lop-sided grin left Buck's face. Stern gravity took its place. He straightened up, moved away from the wall. And he nodded slowly. "Yes," he said. "I am Buck Comstock."

Her hands, trembling a little, were pressed against her lips, while the look which grew in her eyes made Buck shake himself savagely.

"Don't look at me like that," he said harshly. "If Ben Sloan was your uncle, I

95

know what you're thinking. You'd be bound to think that — and I can't blame you. Yet, no matter what lies Jaeger and Cutts might have put in your ears, please remember that there are two sides to everything. I'm not as bad as they've painted me."

"But — but you did — kill Ben Sloan?"

"Yes, I killed him. It was a case of kill or be killed. There was no other out for me. It was one of those things. But of course, you'd never understand."

Again Buck remembered that he was in the open, clear to the sight of anyone who might be looking the ranch over at the moment. So he looked around, searching the distance in every direction. But everywhere the range lay empty, white and hazy under the sun. He took another deep, slow breath and new energy and strength flowed through him. He turned once more to Toad Black, who had not moved. Buck pulled Toad Black's thick wrists behind him and tied them securely with piggin strings. Then he straightened up once more and rolled a cigarette.

He stalked off down to the feed shed and got Black's horse, leading it back to the ranchhouse. Then he waited for Black to regain consciousness. Apparently he had ceased to notice the girl at all. Yet he was aware that she had steadied and quieted, though she was still staring at him with strange eyes.

When Black began to stir, Buck hastened the process with the toe of his boot. Buck caught the fellow by the shoulder, hauled him to a sitting position. Black stayed there, his bloody jaw sagging, stupid daze in his eyes. Buck jabbed a gun in the renegade's ribs. "Get up!" he rasped. "On your feet. You're going with me, Black. And if you try any fuss I won't waste time!"

Toad Black lurched to his feet. There was not a shred of fight or truculence in him now. He was craven and shrunken and a great fear took the place of the daze in his eyes. He was a fearsome sight, with his gashed and bloody face, his swollen, blackened eyes. But there was no fight left in him. Buck took the lariat from the saddle, dropped a loop over Black's head, drew it snug about the beefy throat and tied the other end to the saddle horn. He picked up the reins and was about to swing astride when the girl's hand fell on his arm. Buck turned and faced her. "Well?" he demanded harshly.

She still looked at him with wide eyes, but there was an indefinable difference in the expression of them now to what had been there a few moments before. She spoke with a sort of simple honesty. "Regardless of what else may have happened — at any time — in this, that just took place — well I want to thank you, sincerely. If you had not come to aid me —," she broke off, shuddering.

Some of the bleakness went out of Buck's face. She sure was a handsome little monkey, in spite of her torn blouse and rumpled hair. "Forget it," he said. "Any decent man would have done what I did. And now, if you don't mind — I'll be getting out of here. I can't afford to stay here, in the open. You know why."

She nodded slowly. "Yes. I understand that. What — what are you going to do — with him?" She shivered again, glancing at Toad Black.

"I got use for that hombre," Buck told her. "I'm taking him with me. No — I'm not going to kill him, unless I have to. Though killing is too good for him, at that."

Buck stepped into the saddle, twitched the lariat. "March!" he told Toad Black harshly. "Right up over that ridge yonder."

The girl seemed torn with indecision. Then she called to Buck. "Wait! I want to talk to you, Buck Comstock."

"Sorry," tossed back Buck. "With Brood Shotwell looking for me, I got to get out of sight."

"Then," declared the girl — "I'll ride over that ridge, too."

Buck did not look back, but he knew she was astride the pinto, following him. This was a mix-up, for fair. She had said that Ben Sloan was her uncle. Buck jerked stark and erect in his saddle. If that were so, this girl would be Ben Sloan's heir. She would be the owner of the Wineglass spread! Here was something for the book.

At the top of the ridge Buck made another survey of all the range which fell under his keen and searching gaze. It was bland and peaceful and empty. He rode down the other side to where the Indian grullo pony was grazing, with Toad Black stumbling heavily ahead of him.

"Down on your face," snapped Buck curtly. "Lie down and stay there. I'll be keeping an eye on you. If you try anything, you'll get a slug in you."

Without a word, Toad Black flattened out. He seemed glad of the chance. The girl pulled her pinto horse up beside the other two. She was watching Buck inscrutably. Buck turned to her.

"If you want to talk to me, you'll have to leave your bronc here and climb back to the top of the ridge on foot. I got to keep watch — and it's a good look-out up there."

She did not hesitate. She slid to the ground and marched sturdily along beside him as he climbed up to the screen of wild oats atop the ridge. Buck picked up his Winchester, which he had dropped up there when he charged down on the ranchhouse. He looked back at Toad Black, saw that the fellow was lying quietly by the horses. Buck flattened out and the girl crouched beside him. "Fire away," Buck drawled. "If I don't look at you, don't think I won't be listening. I got to keep on watching."

She was silent for a time. Buck was more aware of her nearness than he would have cared to admit. He darted a glance at her, saw that she was staring at a blade of grass which she kept threading through her fingers. Her red lips were set in troubled, thoughtful lines. She sure was pretty, all right. She drew a deep breath, and spoke suddenly, as though she had made up her mind to take a desperate plunge.

"That was a very brave and unselfish thing to do, Buck Comstock — coming to my aid as you did. For all you knew you might have been driving straight into a situation that could have put you back in — in jail. Yet — you did not hesitate."

Buck stirred restlessly. "I did think of that, but not until I was halfway down to the house. Maybe if the thought had hit me in time, I wouldn't have jumped in so quick. But, when I heard your scream — I didn't stop to think. As it was, everything turned out all right. It's a waste of time thinking about what might have happened. As long as it didn't — forget it. But that wasn't what you wanted to talk to me about."

"No, it wasn't — not altogether." Again she was silent for a time, then with a deep breath, she repeated a question she had blurted at him, down by the house. "You — did kill Ben Sloan?"

"I said I did, didn't I?" rapped Buck.

"Mur— murdered him?"

"No!" said Buck explosively. "No, I didn't murder him. In this country, when a man has to kill in defense of his own life — it isn't called murder — and it isn't murder. That is what I did. Ben Sloan came for me, rolling smoke. I did only what any other sane person would do. I shot to keep from being shot. Ben Sloan missed. I didn't. And that is the truth, if it was ever spoken."

"But the jury —."

"Toad Black, that damned animal that was after you — he was on the jury. Would you take his word — or anything, now that you know what he's like?"

"I see," she said slowly. "I see. I did overhear some talk — where the word railroaded was used. And there was that big white-haired man in the courtroom who defied the Judge and said that it was all a farce, a crooked set-up. I — I believe you, Buck Comstock."

There was no particular reason why these words should have made Buck feel good. Yet they did. He turned his head and smiled at her, and that smile held an intriguing suggestion of boyishness in it. "That's swell. I'm mighty glad to have you say that, Miss —."

She colored slightly, but did not miss the cue. "Harper," she said. "Jean Harper. I — I wanted to make sure of things, for there is much I do not understand. You see, Ben Sloan was not really my uncle, except by law. He was the only brother of my dead step-father. At that, as far as I know, I'm the only living kin of Ben Sloan."

"Which makes you owner of the Wineglass spread?" asked Buck softly.

"Apparently. I really had no idea that Ben Sloan owned any property — or any idea where he even was — nor if he was still alive. I had almost forgotten him. And then, Mr. Jaeger got in touch with me and advised me to come out here —."

"And now," broke in Buck — "Jaeger wants to buy the Wineglass spread from you. Right?"

She looked at him keenly. "How did you know?"

Buck laughed mirthlessly. "Because that would be exactly in line with what he's scheming to do. How much did he offer you for the place?"

She hesitated, her lips tightening. "I don't know that I should —."

"Of course," growled Buck. "I forgot for a minute that I was an outlaw. I got no right to ask that. But let me give you a little good advice, though. Before you sell to anybody, you go get the help of some reliable cattleman on the proposition. Somebody who knows range, knows cattle and who will give you a square deal. If you don't, Jaeger and Cutts will rob you blind. You don't have to take my word for it that they're a pair of cut-throats and shysters. There's a war on between me and them and you'd naturally figure I was a little prejudiced. So you go have a talk with Bill Morgan or Johnny Frazier or Bud Tharp. There are three four square, honest men, who'll give you a fair and square estimate on what you should get for your spread."

The girl stared thoughtfully at the ground, her smooth brow corrugated in a frown. Then she spoke impulsively, a delightful smile touching her lips. "I'm a suspicious little idiot. I'm sorry, Buck Comstock. Tell me — what would you say the Wineglass ranch is worth?"

"Not a cent less than twenty thousand dollars," Buck answered tersely.

"Twenty thousand dollars!" She stared at him aghast. "Why Mr. Jaeger only offered six thousand — but I thought that was an awful lot of money."

"It is a lot of money, until you mention it as a price against the Wineglass. Then it is chickenfeed — downright robbery. Me, I don't know exactly how many cattle are packing the Wineglass iron, but I got a reasonable idea. And I do know about how much range it takes in, what kind of range it is and what the possibilities of that range are. I ought to know, for my own ranch, the Half Moon joins the Wineglass on the south. I say again, you wouldn't be getting a cent too much at twenty thousand."

Buck twisted around and took another look down into the hollow at Toad Black. The renegade was still there, quite evidently convinced that in this particular spot, discretion was the better part of foolishness.

The girl was obviously disturbed and impressed by Buck's words and tone. If the price he had put on her ranch was even remotely correct, then indeed had Jaeger and Cutts intended to, as Buck Comstock had naively put it, rob her blind. She furtively studied this lean young cowboy beside her. He was staring out across the range again, his sun blackened jaw jutting and firm, his lips compressed in serious vigilance. His eyes held that far, keen fire of a hunting hawk. Relaxed as he was she could see the lean, tough, muscular grace of him, a pantherish certainty and poise about him. And she remembered him as he had crushed a bigger and heavier foe in blasting, tigerish fury. He didn't look like a killer or a murderer to Jean Harper. He looked like a clean cut, attractive rider who was still resplendent with youth, but who carried certain lines of maturity about his mouth and chin. He looked like a man who could be trusted.

"I suppose," she said quietly — "you're wondering why I wanted to come up here and speak to you. Particularly so in the light of — well, when you admit you came off victor in a shooting scrape with my uncle."

"That's right," nodded Buck. "I am."

"I'll tell you," she said, in sudden decision. "At first it was pure impulse, impulse born of the fact that you did — what you did in saving me from that animal. It was that, and also that I've been desperately anxious to talk with someone who knows this country and the values of ranches in it. There — there is something about you, Buck Comstock — which invites confidence. I suppose I should fear you, hate you — if only for the memory of Ben Sloan. But I don't and I can't. After all, Ben Sloan was little more than a name to me. I only saw him once in my life, and that was many, many years ago when I was just a little girl. I cannot even recall what he looked like now. He is just a dim, shadowy remembrance to me — part of the past which has just about faded out. So, I find myself unable to become overly concerned with his death, even though it did react to my benefit. He is a vague unreality to me — more like a half forgotten name than anything else. May— maybe that doesn't sound very clear to you. And I don't want you to think that I am heartless. But I am speaking honestly and with no false sentiment."

"I understand," drawled Buck. He was thinking that this girl would always be honest and straightforward. She had that knack about her. Deceit simply wasn't in her.

"Yes," she said. "I simply had to talk to someone. For you see — I do not trust either Mr. Jaeger or Mr. Cutts."

"Good girl," enthused Buck. "You got savvy. Go on."

She did, thoughtfully. "Even from the very first it struck me as strange that Jaeger and Cutts, both total strangers to me, should go to the time and trouble of having me traced, so that they could notify me of this inheritance. I know human nature enough to realize that people don't, as a rule, do those things merely from the goodness of their hearts. It struck me as perfectly obvious that Jaeger and Cutts had done this in the hope of making a personal profit from it somewhere. Therefore, when I first met them I was on my guard and felt little confidence in them. Also, even though six thousand dollars loomed as an awful lot to me, there was something about Leek Jaeger when he made the offer — an eagerness, a greedy eagerness and a filmed cunning in his eyes that I did not miss.

"I told him I would think the proposition over, and since then have asked them several times to take me out here to the Wineglass so that I might look the place over. But always both of them have had some excuse for not doing so. One of their arguments, since your escape from jail, was that you were on the loose and they would have had me believe that you were some terrifying dragon or destroyer who might eat alive any woman you met up with. Their excuses were hardly convincing so today I managed to slip away from the J Bar C — both Jaeger and Cutts having gone to town. I met up with a cowboy out on the range and asked him how to get to the Wineglass headquarters. He put me on the right trail. You know the rest."

"It all fits in with the rest of the picture," mused Buck softly. "Yeah, it fits perfect." He looked directly into the girl's questing, measuring eyes and spoke crisply. "Miss Harper, I know Leek Jaeger and Frank Cutts a lot better than you do. I know them for exactly what they are. There's neither truth or honor in either one of them. They would double-cross their own mother — or skin a flea for its hide and tallow. Right now you're staying at the J Bar C, a guest there. I'm advising you to leave, right away. Go into town and stay at Joe Lester's hotel. If you intend to sell the Wineglass, let a competent lawyer handle the proposition for you. I can recommend Curt Wallace. He's young, but he's as square as a die — and no man's fool. If you think you'd like to hold on to your ranch, to go into the cattle business — get in touch with Bill Morgan and ask his advice. They don't come any better than Bill and he's forgot more about the cattle game than most men will ever know. He's been raising cattle for the better part of fifty years and he knows the game both ways from the ace. If you follow his advice you can't go wrong. And old Bill is just one of those fine and rare men who'd be more than glad to help you out any way he could."

The girl stared out into the distance for some little time. Then she nodded slowly. "Thanks, Buck Comstock. I'll do as you say. Now — I'll be riding. As I said before, I should hate and fear you. But — I don't. And thanks again, both for what you did for me, down at the ranchhouse, and for the fine, fair counsel you've given me."

"Call it even, all the way around," smiled Buck. "Shake?"

She hesitated, matched his smile and held out her hand. She had a swell smile, thought Buck. It went with the rest of her. This girl was the pure quill. You bet!

"You might," drawled Buck — "say nothing to anybody about meeting me out here. I'm still on the dodge, but I reckon there'll maybe come a time when I won't be."

He still held her hand. "Of course," she nodded, color building up in her face at the pressure of his lean, brown paw. "I understand. Goodbye, Buck Comstock."

"I hope you're wrong there," said Buck gravely. "I hope it isn't — goodbye. Rather make it — hasta la vista — until we meet again."

CHAPTER FIVE

Shortly before midnight, Buck Comstock was again on the prowl. On foot he was reconnoitering the Circle Star. Well back from the ranchhouse, out on the empty range, two ground-reined horses stood quietly, while in the dewy grass beside them lay Toad Black, firmly tied, hand and foot.

The Circle Star ranchhouse was dark and quiet, so Buck finally worked his way again up to the window of the cook's back room, where he knocked softly at the glass. After a time he succeeded in rousing Bones Baker, who slid the window cautiously up. "Quien es — who is it?" demanded Bones in a hoarse whisper. "That you again, Buck?"

"Right, Bones. Let me in. I want to talk to Bill."

The three of them gathered in the cook's room and Bones hung a blanket over the window before lighting a lamp. "Can't run no chances of having Brood Shotwell or that sour-puss deputy of his peekin' in on us," puffed Bones.

"I got news for you, Bill," said Buck abruptly.

"That goes double, kid," boomed Morgan softly. "I got news for you, too. You remember that girl that was with Jaeger and Cutts in the courtroom, Buck? Well, she's —."

"Ben Sloan's heir," cut in Buck, grinning.

Bill Morgan stared at him. "How the hell did you find that out? Who you been talking to?"

"Had a long talk with the lady herself, today," Buck drawled. "Listen while I tell you how it happened."

He told the story of the afternoon's happenings in brief, terse words. "And," he ended — "I told her to get loose from Jaeger and Cutts and stay at the hotel in town. I told her to let Curt Wallace handle her affairs and to call on you for advice, Bill. She promised she would do it. Tomorrow you ram right into town and have a talk with her."

"I'll do it, of course," Morgan nodded. "But you — if you ain't got the damnedest knack of bumping into things."

"What did you do with Toad Black?"

asked Bones eagerly. "Take him out and kill him, Buck?"

"Hardly," chuckled Buck. "You, I'm afraid, got awful bloody ideas, Bones."

"I shore have, in a case like that," asserted Bones stoutly. "He shore needed killing, treating that pore girl the way he did. Me, I could kill a jasper like that and feel plumb satisfied with myself. But if you didn't kill him — what did you do with him?"

"Coming to that. Dead, Toad Black wouldn't be worth a plugged dime to anybody. Alive, he can be made to talk. I got sense enough to realize that I can't keep on dodging Brood Shotwell forever. Somewhere along the line he'd be shore to catch up with me. So, if it can possibly be managed, I got to clear myself according to law. I got no yen to keep on playing scared coyote all my life, out in Big Sage Desert. Well, if I can prove that some member of that jury — Toad Black or any of the others, was approached by Jaeger or Cutts and was paid or bribed to vote me guilty no matter what the evidence said, then the whole trial would have to be thrown out and I could get a new shake. But I can't keep on dragging Black around with me, not while I'm on the dodge. I got to leave him somewhere in safe keeping. That's where you two come in. How about it, can you take care of him for me?"

It was Bones Baker who answered. "You bet! Bring him in, cowboy. I'll keep him in my spud cellar. How about it, Boss?"

Bill Morgan grinned and nodded. "Think you can handle him, Bones?"

"Handle him!" Bones snorted. "Wait and see. He tries getting ructious with me and I'll pin his ears back, plenty. I'd take supreme delight in currying that hombre with a pick handle two or three times a day. You bet — lead me to him."

Bill Morgan went out with Buck to bring in the horses and Toad Black. Bones swore in sublime amazement as he viewed Black's face. "Holy hen-hawks!" he exploded. "You must have had a rock in each fist, Buck. Don't try and tell me you never used anything on him but your hands."

"It's a wonder I didn't bust my hands all to hell and gone," Buck grinned. "He was plenty tough, what I mean. He took an awful lot of slapping around before he went down to stay. Okay, Bones — he's all yours."

Toad Black scowled savagely around through his swollen, blackened eyes. "You hombres — all three of you — shore are storing up plenty of trouble for yourselves," he growled thickly. "You can't treat a white man in this way and get by with it."

Bones bristled truculently. "You're no white man. You're all striped polecat. Just one little word on how you treated that girl today — just one little word to some of the boys, and you'd be stretching a hemp necktie before you could think twice." Bones pulled his big six-shooter out of his blankets and waved it suggestively. "Starting now," he proclaimed — "one side-winder known as Toad Black, disappears from the world and ken of men. March — you plug ugly blister, and do exactly as you're told. Else you'll think all hell and half of purgatory is crawling your frame."

Jean Harper knew a big sense of relief when she returned to the J Bar C headquarters and found that Jaeger and Cutts were still in town. There were several punchers down around the corrals, but she rode in with her right side away from them, so that they would not see that her right arm was bare, that a sleeve had been torn from her silk blouse. She did not stop at the corrals to leave her pinto, for she knew someone would take care of the animal even if she did leave it in front of the ranchhouse.

She realized that she could not afford to have any questions asked her as to what had happened, and why her blouse was torn as it was. Hence her relief on finding the ranchhouse empty as she hurried to the room that had been given her by Leek Jaeger. There she stripped off the offending blouse, wadded it up and thrust it into a far corner of one of her traveling bags. She had a cold bath and viewed with shudders of repugnant memory, the dark bruises on the soft flesh of her arms and shoulders where the clawing fingers of Toad Black had touched.

Yet, right after this repugnance, came a warm and truant thrill. She was thinking of Buck Comstock — of the flaming, savage ferocity of him as he had beaten down Toad Black. This thrill made her feel a little guilty. Instead of thrilling over the thought of that lean cowboy, she should have known a certain fear and dislike, if not of hate. For he had killed her uncle, Ben Sloan — and had admitted it. He had been found guilty of murder by a jury of riding men and he had been sentenced to twenty-five years in a penitentiary. He had broken jail, was a hunted man — an outlaw. Yes, by all accepted standards she should know nothing but aversion at the mere thought of Buck Comstock.

In the world that Jean Harper had lived in, all of these things would have put a man so far beyond the pale, no decent person would give him even a kind thought. This, however, was apparently a different kind of world, out here in the far flung plains and deserts of the cattle country — an entirely different world, where men and their acts were gauged and measured by an entirely new set of standards. Out here it would seem, a man could kill in self-defense and have his act judged entirely justifiable by many citizens. And it would leave no stain upon him whatever.

Dimly, for there was still a great deal more for her to learn and unlearn about this western country, Jean Harper could perceive something of the spirit and elemental reasoning of the cattleland. Already it was affecting her, opening her eyes, widening her perceptions. In one thing, of course, there was no difference between this world and the one she had previously lived in. Men were much alike, fundamentally. Some were honest, some dishonest — some good and some bad — some brave and others cowardly.

It had, Jean Harper mused, taken a lot of courage to do as Buck Comstock had done — to forget his own dangerous circumstances entirely and leap generously to the aid of a total stranger. That had taken, not only courage, but a certain fine and honest chivalry. That act might have cost him his liberty, even his life. Yet he had not hesitated. Surely no man who would do as Buck Comstock had done could be really vicious or without principle.

The girl's eyes shone warmly as she pictured those terrific moments. What a literal tiger of a man he had been, as he smashed Toad Black into insensibility. And she could see Buck Comstock plainly as he had been just before she left him — the lean, hard, muscular brownness of his face and jaw — the alert, cool clearness of his grey eyes, eyes which crinkled at the corners when he smiled.

And then there were all of those personal things she had told him. A total stranger, whom she had met for the first time in her life, and she had confided in him! Of course, impulse had had something to do with that — impulse born of the emotional hurricane she had been through. Yet there must also have been some instinctive realization of honor and trust in the man's make-up. It was all very strange and bewildering. At the moment Jean Harper was not entirely certain that she knew even herself.

It was after dark when Leek Jaeger and Frank Cutts returned to the ranch. Jaeger was plainly out of sorts as he came stamping into the house, but Cutts, whatever his feelings were, masked them behind that cold, set, pale gambler's face of his.

Jean Harper had already eaten and she came into the dining room just as the two partners finished their evening meal. At her entrance Leek Jaeger's head jerked up and his eyes held a real impact as they reached her.

"I understand you took a long ride this afternoon," Jaeger growled. "And I thought I told you not to go gallivanting here and yon around this range."

Jean drew herself up coldly. "As your guest, Mr. Jaeger — I fail to understand either your tone or your meaning. Are you trying to tell me that I am subject to your orders?"

Hot blood congested Leek Jaeger's heavy face. It took a very obvious effort on his part to swallow the words that were on his lips, and to substitute less offensive ones.

"I didn't mean it exactly that way, Miss Harper," he blurted. "Only — you're out here as a guest of Frank and me and we naturally feel a responsibility for your safety. You don't know the kind of country this is, or the kind of men in it. You shouldn't go on long rides alone."

Frank Cutts nodded. "Leek is right, Miss Harper," he said in his cold, measured tones. "This country is entirely too wild and rough for a girl like you to ride about it without escort."

Standing half in, half out of the lamp glow at the moment, Jean Harper was a decidedly handsome picture. She had donned a soft, grey dress — a simple thing of flowing lines which brought out the cool, clean, girlish slenderness of her. Her erect dark head was touched with glints of dusted gold by the lamplight, and there was quick color in her cheeks.

Cutts, looking at her, knew a sudden stirring of pulse. For a brief second the practiced curtain of his eyes lowered and something of the cold, calculating, unscrupulous interior of the man leered out. "No," he spoke again, his voice less chill and brittle than before. "We wouldn't want anything to happen to you."

Guarded and swift as had been that lowering of the curtain in Cutts' eyes, Jean had seen and recognized the treacherous, turgid soul of the man. A little shiver ran up her spine. But she kept her head high.

"You can rest your fears," she said coldly. "I can take care of myself. And that ride I took today was really very enlightening. Oh — very much so."

Both Cutts and Jaeger jerked their heads forward, their eyes boring at her. "So—o!" murmured Jaeger. "And just where did you ride to?"

"Out to my ranch, the Wineglass. And what I saw certainly opened my eyes to a great many things."

This shot also told. Jaeger licked his lips and glanced at Cutts. Then his eyes came back to Jean. "Such as — what?" he demanded.

Spots of anger began to dance in Jean's cheeks. She grew a little reckless. "For one thing, it made me realize that the offer you made of six thousand dollars was a downright swindle. To get the Wineglass for six thousand would be just like stealing it."

Jaeger tried to laugh, but the effort produced more of a croak than anything else. "What do you know about range and cattle values in this country?" he scoffed. "By your own admission this is the first time you were ever in country like this. I'm telling you that the Wineglass ain't worth a red penny more than six thousand dollars. Even that is a generous offer."

"I may be a stranger to this country," retorted Jean spiritedly. "But I'm not an entire fool. You, or no one else will ever buy the Wineglass from me for six thousand dollars — or anything near that amount. For one thing, I can understand why you always had some excuse for not taking me out to look the place over. You knew that I would realize something of the real value of the property and you were anxious to swindle me by getting me to sell at your figure. Well, I'm no child and I think you've found it out."

Cutts spoke and his voice seemed just a little tighter than usual. "I'm inclined to agree with Leek as to the real value of the ranch, Miss Harper. But I resent your implication that we were trying to put anything over on you. Just to show you how wrong you are in that impression, Leek and I will jump that offer fifteen hundred dollars. That is seventy-five hundred for the ranch."

Jean shrugged, shaking her head. "You might as well realize that I don't intend to sell my ranch. Instead I am going to operate it myself. I'm going into the cattle raising business."

"You!" ejaculated Leek Jaeger. "You — run the Wineglass on your own! You — go into the cattle business!" He leaned back and laughed. "Don't be a fool, girl — don't be a fool."

Jean stood very straight, her face going white with indignant anger. "Mr. Jaeger, I distinctly resent your tone and manner. Anyone would think that you had some kind of authority over me. You haven't — not a bit. You make it impossible for me to remain in this house any longer. The first thing in the morning, I am removing to town, to the hotel."

She turned then and swept from the room. In the distance of the house the door of her room closed, emphatically. Frank Cutts looked at Leek Jaeger in swift anger and disgust. "Sometimes I wonder just how in hell you ever got as far along in this world as you have, Leek. I admit that you got some brains, but at a time like to-night, any man would doubt it. You sure made a mess of that."

"I don't see it," bawled Jaeger angrily. "I only —."

Cutts spread his hands in exaggerated weariness. "Oh, let's not row among ourselves. We can't afford to. But you never will admit that you're wrong. Yet you've been wrong in several ways lately. The big blunder was when you tried to proposition Buck Comstock that night in jail. If you'd have stayed away, he'd have been in Pinole by this time and things would have begun to quiet down. But no — you got a wild idea and you spread our hand right in front of him — showed him every card. Comstock is nobody's fool. That's another mistake you always make. You never give the other fellow credit for having any savvy. You think nobody can see through your deals but yourself. Buck Comstock did, plenty. He had a desperate play for a getaway as soon as you spread your cards. He got away. He's got friends — damned powerful friends. You can bet he's seen some of them, talked with them. Why have Morgan and Frazier and Tharp all sent out calls for extra riders? They're not branding or rounding up. Yet they're taking on hands every day. I know the answer and so do you. They realize what our plans are. And it's all your fault. You laid those plans wide out when you went to see Comstock in the jail."

"All right — all right," Jaeger snarled. "Let it go at that. I dragged my rope on that play. But this damn girl — what are we going to do about her? I'm wondering damn hard where Toad Black was, when she was out at the Wineglass. We sent him out there special to keep anyone from snooping around the place. And you can't tell me that girl has savvy enough to make any intelligent guess as to what a piece of this range is worth. She's had a talk with somebody — you bet she has. I'd shore give a lot to know who it was."

Cutts shrugged. "Whatever happened, all I know for certain right now is this — you've made her mad — mighty mad. And once she leaves this ranch, there won't be only one person to talk to her — there'll be plenty of them. Maybe she made the rounds today and talked to a whole flock of them. Anyway, you can see that she'd definitely made up her mind not to sell the Wineglass — at least, not to us. What's the answer?"

"I'll bite," grunted Jaeger. "What is it? Men, I know how to handle. But a damned obstreperous, stubborn, high headed filly like her — I'm damned if I know what to do about it."

Cutts stood up, took a couple of turns about the room. "All my life I've gambled," he said slowly. "I've never dodged the stakes, no matter how high they went. And whenever I picked up a hand and decided to back it — I backed it to the limit. We've picked up a hand here. It's not as strong now as when the first bets went down. But I'm backing this hand we hold. I'm going to play it to the limit. I'll bet as long as my chips last — and then I'll bluff. When bluffing ceases to bring in chips, why then I'll fight, to the last damned step. In other words, the thing we've worked and planned to do, is going to be done. Possession of the Wineglass spread is vital to all we hope for. We've got to have it. Without it, we're right back where we started a year ago, when we first made our plans. So, we'll get the Wineglass. That girl has got to change her mind — she's going to change her mind. I'm telling you something."

Jaeger was staring at his partner. He could not remember ever seeing Frank Cutts in exactly this frame of mind before. There was something about Cutts at this moment which made Jaeger realize that he had never really known Frank Cutts before.

"That won't be as easy as it sounds," argued Jaeger uneasily. "She ain't got that haughty chin for nothing. And she's leaving us in the morning."

"No," said Cutts softly — "no, she's not going to leave us, Leek."

Jaeger lit a black cheroot. "Go on," he purred softly.

Cutts spoke in low, swift tones, emphasizing his words with little jerky motions of his hands. When he had finished, Leek Jaeger sat for some time, motionless, his heavy features set, his little, leaden eyes staring and unwinking. Presently he cleared his throat, with a harsh, rasping sound. "That will mean all of our chips go on one hand," he said thickly. "Hell will split wide open if there's any kind of a slip."

"There won't be any slip," said Cutts. "Not if you'll keep your mouth shut and let me handle this. No man ever made a plan work if he lost his guts and stopped half way. And no plan ever works as smooth as it first figures out. Yet we still hold high cards if we got nerve to back 'em — all the way."

"It will stir up an awful row," said Jaeger. "We'll have this whole damned range on our necks if anybody once guesses the truth."

"Can you think of a better plan?" Cutts demanded impatiently.

"No," admitted Jaeger — "I can't." He nodded in sudden decision. "Fair enough. I'll go you."

A few minutes later a knock sounded on the door of Jean Harper's room. "This is Cutts, Miss Harper. Could Mr. Jaeger and I see you for another minute? Leek is sorry he spoke as he did. We'd like to talk over another proposition with you."

Jean was of two minds for a moment. Somehow her distrust of the two men had grown enormously since her meeting with Buck Comstock. And with her own eyes, while talking to these men but a few minutes before, she had seen the curtain raise enough to disclose the greed and unscrupulousness of their natures.

She would have preferred to have neither seen nor heard anything of them, ever again.

However, she was keen enough of wit to realize that anything additional of their scheming plans which she might learn now, would perhaps come in handy later on. There could be no harm in listening to what they had to propose. If they were seeking in some way to outwit her, she'd show them that she could fence a little herself. She opened the door.

"I'm perfectly willing to hear what you

may have to say," she told Cutts. "Providing I do not have to hear any more insults from Jaeger."

"There'll be none," promised Cutts. "Leek is a rough and tough old hombre, and his tongue runs away with him at times. But he really means nothing by it. Right now he's all broken up because of hurting your feelings."

As Cutts walked beside her, it came to Jean that there was something of the prowl of a jungle animal in his stride. A strange man, this fellow Cutts, with that cold, emotionless face of his. But Jean felt that she had read him correctly. Beneath that frozen faced poise of his, there was a great capacity of evil in Frank Cutts. Of that, Jean was certain. An overwhelming aversion to him gripped her.

At the door of the dining room Cutts paused to let Jean enter ahead of him. In there was Leek Jaeger, holding a colorful Navajo blanket in his hands, examining some of its figuration. As Jean entered, Jaeger looked up with what was plainly meant as a placating grin. He held the blanket out to her.

"Here's a peace offering, Miss Harper," he said. "I'm apologizing for speaking to you as I did. I been so used to ordering around a leather eared bunch of cow punchers, I kinda forget myself at times. So please accept this blanket with my compliments."

Jean, a trifle taken back, was non-plussed for a moment. She hesitated, then stepped forward, her hands outstretched. "Thank you, Mr. Jaeger. This is kind of you."

The next moment the arms of Frank Cutts dropped about her, tightening like rawhide withes, clamping her own arms tight against her sides, holding her powerless. And Jaeger, with a move lightning fast for one of his stodgy bulk, flung the blanket over her head, drawing the heavy folds across her face and throat, stifling and muffling any instinctive outcry she might have made.

For a moment Jean was too dumbfounded, too startled to make move or sound. Then a white fury at the deceit and trickery of these two rascals swept over her. She began to fight and struggle like some trapped wild thing. Slender as she was, Jean Harper was no weakling. She twisted and writhed and squirmed. As her hands were powerless she used her feet and landed a lusty kick on Leek Jaeger's knee cap that set him to yelping and cursing with pain. He let go of the blanket and

Jean shook her head from side to side, trying to rid herself of it.

Frank Cutts, cursing savagely at Jaeger, tightened the pressure of his arms until Jean thought her spine must break. Darts of agony went through her. Jaeger, coming back ferociously, padded the blanket about her face and head until she could hardly breathe. The strength went out of her and she sagged limply. A moment later, blinded, half smothered by the blanket, arms and ankles tightly bound, Jean lay helpless on the floor.

It seemed for a time that her senses would surely leave her. Short as the time had been since Cutts first seized her until this moment when she lay helpless, she had put forth every ounce of strength she had possessed in her battle to win free. Now the reaction had set in and she felt weak and sick and dazed — almost stupefied by the suddenness and brutality of it all. For some time Jean swam through the mists which only dimly separated reality and unconsciousness.

Slowly her wits and a little thread of courage came back to her. What was the meaning of this thing — the purpose of it? What plan had these two treacherous, cowardly brutes figured out? Leek Jaeger, with his blocky, sullen features, his little, lead colored, brutal eyes. Frank Cutts, with his cold emotionless face who had just once raised the curtain of his eyes long enough for Jean to glimpse the turgid, evil soul beyond. Of a sudden the strange, wavering madness of hysteria began tugging at the girl's throat. She was alone — and so utterly, utterly helpless —.

That hysteria strained at Jean's lips and her lips parted. But the incipient scream was never uttered. Cold reason broke through and ordered her jangled senses. A whisper of new courage reached out and touched her. The whisper grew stronger until it became a live current. It cooled the fire of dread in her and she relaxed, the slim lines of her body softening from the rigid, hard tenseness which had convulsed her. Muffled though her head was in that blanket, she could hear Jaeger and Cutts talking.

"Go get the horses, Leek," Cutts ordered. "I'll keep watch here. And if any of those punchers down at the bunkhouse should see you and ask questions, pass it off that we're riding to town with the girl. Maybe they wouldn't give a damn anyhow, even if they knew the truth. But you never can tell, and some of them might make talk. Hurry up."

Jean heard Jaeger depart. A door slammed shut. Momentary silence settled in. Then Cutts stepped close to her. "If you play the game and do as you're told, you won't be hurt," he said. "But if you turn into an obstreperous fool, you'll be calmed down in a hurry and in a way that won't be exactly pleasant."

She heard Cutts leave the room. For a moment the wild thought of possible escape came to her. But it quickly dissipated. Those bonds about her wrists and ankles were drawn cruelly tight. Strain and pull as she might, she could not win even the slightest bit of slack. She relaxed again, panting and shivering, dizzy for a good full breath of air which the blanket denied her.

Cutts was soon back and Jean could tell that he was anxious and restless, for he kept pacing the floor nervously, back and forth — back and forth. Jean heard a match snap as Cutts lighted a cigarette and then, even through the blanket she could smell the tobacco smoke.

A distant door slammed, footsteps echoed. Came Jaeger's voice, exultant. "Couple of heavy poker games going on in the bunkhouse. Nobody prowling around outside, nobody interested in what we do, Frank. Nobody saw or heard me get the broncs. This will work as smooth as you please. Everything set? Come on, then. You grab her feet."

Hands settled on Jean's ankles, on her shoulders. She was lifted and carried out, her body swaying as the two men walked. A current of cool air touched her hands and wrists and she knew she was out of the house. She heard a horse stamp and snort gustily. She was lowered to the ground. Someone fumbled at the tie about her ankles. Then came the voice of Cutts again, low and smooth and suave, but deadly cold.

"You're going to be put on a horse, tied in the saddle. You haven't a ghost of a chance to get away. You'll only make unnecessary trouble for yourself if you try. Use an ounce of common sense and you'll be all right."

Her ankles were freed and she was lifted into a saddle. Then her ankles were tied once more, this time to the cinch rings on both sides of the saddle. Her wrists were thonged to the saddle horn. And the blanket was tied in place about her head and throat. The two rascals were making certain that she would have no idea just where she was taken to. Then the horse beneath her began to move.

CHAPTER SIX

For the next two or three days, following his delivery of Toad Black to the belligerent care of Bones Baker at the Circle Star, Buck Comstock passed no word with any human being. He spent most of his time well back in the vast shelter of Big Sage Desert. No two times did he camp in the same place. Each tiny fire he built for the cooking of food, spread its ashes where no other ashes had ever been before, and each time Buck lay down to sleep his blankets covered earth never touched by blankets before.

Long hours each day he spent with a pair of binoculars given him by Bill Morgan. He studied miles and miles of the surrounding country, alert to every foreign movement or sign of riders. Twice he did see riders, far out in the coiling mists of mirage and each time, leading them, was a man on a big, red horse. Buck knew that horse. It belonged to Brood Shotwell.

Shotwell was the stubborn, tenacious

man-hunter all right, all right. He was like a bull-dog, once he set his teeth into a job. But human ability had its limitations, even when backed up by the kind of dogged persistence possessed by Brood Shotwell. This time he was up against a fugitive who could lay false trails and blot out real ones and at no time did Shotwell and his posses ever get close enough to cause Buck any real uneasiness.

Out there in the desert, Buck had plenty of time for thought through long, blazing days and equally long, chill, lonely nights. Guarded by the solitude and stillness, Buck's concentration became such that he saw the scheme of Jaeger and Cutts with steadily growing clearness and his convictions as to the ultimate purpose of the two men became utterly set.

Not all of his thoughts however, centered about Jaeger and Cutts. With increasing frequency Jean Harper intruded in his musings. It gave him a strange, warm pleasure to think of her. Again and again he lived over those momentous minutes when he had tossed caution to the winds and raced down that slope to her rescue. At these times it seemed that he could again feel the impact of his clenched fists as they had ripped into

Toad Black's brutal face and gross body. He knew a savage satisfaction in the fact that he had beaten Black down, that he had punished the renegade terribly. And he remembered Jean Harper as she had looked when he turned away from the prone and senseless Black. Her hair had been tousled, her blouse torn, the flesh of her bare arm darkening with bruises, and terrific relief in her eyes with the knowledge that the danger had passed.

His first impulse had been to comfort her, much as he would a frightened, weeping child. But she had recognized him then and had drawn away, quick horror in her eyes again as she realized that he was the man who had killed Ben Sloan, her uncle.

Yet, before she had left him, she had shown a remarkable display of common sense. She had viewed the death of Ben Sloan with open mind and seemed to understand that in the provocation which lay behind the fatal gun play, Buck had had no other out than the one he had taken. And after that the barriers had really broken down and she had talked fairly with him, really confided in him, and had agreed to accept his advice about her ranch problem. And she had left him as a friend, promising to tell no one that she had met and talked with him, out there at the Wineglass head-quarters.

These thoughts gave Buck a lot of satisfaction during the lonely hours of his exile. They made the heat of the sun seem less blasting and defeated the utter loneliness of the far, wild nights. It seemed, when you had something definite to tie to, like memories of this sort, a fellow could isolate himself from his surroundings and live in a world of fancy. But the more Buck thought of Jean Harper, the more he knew an ever growing desire to see her and speak to her again — this girl with the ebon hair and the enchanting slimness —the honest eyes and lips.

He wondered if Bill Morgan had been able to see her and talk to her. Or maybe Curt Wallace, who had a mighty good head on him, despite the fact that he was young. Lucky dogs they were, mused Buck — if they had basked in the quick warmth of her smile. While he — well, he slunk around this damned desert like a hunted coyote. He thought that if he could not see her again, it would help a lot to hear some news of her. The old reckless impetuosity took hold of him. It was about time he took a chance and paid another visit to the Circle Star.

So it was, that in the thick, warm dusk of the third day, Buck once more rode cautiously down upon the Circle Star headquarters. As before, he left the little grullo pony well back from the buildings and went in on foot, cautious and stealthy. There were several lights about the place, for it was too early for Bill and his outfit to turn in yet.

Abruptly Buck halted, flattened out to dead stillness, melting into the shadows along the ground. In front of the Circle Star ranchhouse were many horses and many men.

Buck's mind raced. Why were these men there — and who were they? Had something happened to Bill Morgan? Had Jaeger and Cutts already started their projected invasion of Coyote Valley range and were the riders of the Coyote Valley ranches gathered here to organize for battle? Or was it Brood Shotwell who was there — Shotwell and a posse? Maybe Toad Black had escaped and reported to Shotwell, bringing the sheriff down on Bill Morgan's neck because of Bill's friendliness and willingness to protect the man Shotwell was after. A thousand possible conjectures whipped through Buck's brain. But there was no coherent answer available while he lay out there in the dark. If he wanted to find out what was going on there was only one answer. He had to get in closer.

It was hard, ramming around in the dark, both figuratively and literally as he was, when his heart and interests were bound up so tightly with Bill Morgan and the rest of the Faithful. Daring decision took hold of Buck. He got back to his feet and circled the house, a noiseless, low-crouched shadow.

Buck knew the Circle Star ranchhouse well enough. On the blind side of the house he tried two windows, found the second partially open. With slow, steady pressure he pushed the sash up far enough to wriggle through. Once inside he sat down and pulled off his boots. Then he began feeling his way from room to room. On the far side of the second room he explored was a door with lines of yellow light drawn across the top and bottom. Buck crept in close to that door, pressed his ear to it and listened. Voices were speaking in the next room. Buck recognized Brood Shotwell's cold, heavy tones.

Buck was startled, but not overly alarmed. It was hardly possible that Shotwell would even dream that the man he had been trailing so relentlessly was in this very ranchhouse with him — less than a dozen yards distant at this very moment. Buck had to grin at the ironical features of the set-up. He eased a belt gun into his hand, just in case, and settled himself to listen.

"This range has gone completely loco, I tell you, Morgan," Shotwell was saying. "First was the trouble with Comstock. Now Toad Black has disappeared, complete. And that girl — the Harper girl — she's vanished into thin air. Nobody knows anything, nobody has seen anything. At least that's what they claim. Wonder what in hell will happen next. Damned if I ain't beginning to get a little spooky, myself."

Bill Morgan's deep voice answered him. "Toad Black don't count at all, Brood. He was only a drifter at best, not worth the powder and lead to blow his head off. Most likely, realizing that he shared the responsibility of the damnedest legal farce I ever heard of — or that you did either, and fearing that retribution might pop up and lay hands on him any time, he just simply hightailed it out of this country complete."

"You're still hacking away at that Comstock trial, ain't you?" rasped the sheriff.

"Can't get that out of your craw?"

"I shore can't," growled Morgan. "What decent man could? Listen here, Brood. You've grown old and grey, dealing with the faults and meannesses of human beings. You've been present at more than one trial. You've seen how they were run — fair trials, I mean. You know the different kinds of evidence and what it is worth. Right now you can't look me square in the eye and tell me that Buck Comstock got a fair shake in that trial."

"My office ain't concerned with that angle of law enforcement," grunted Shotwell. "All I'm supposed to do is round up the jasper the warrant calls for and then do with him whatever the court tells me to do. My authority goes only so far and then ends right there. What I personally think, one way or the other about a case, doesn't mean a damned thing. I know that, so I keep my mouth shut. I might think a prisoner is innocent or that he's guilty. But if the court says otherwise — well, that's all there is to it. I got no time arguing about Comstock. And I might say I'm not sprouting any grey hairs over the disappearance of Toad Black. Maybe you're right about him. Maybe he did drift out of the country, knowing that Comstock was

142

on the loose and liable to meet up with him some time. Either way, that don't matter. It's this girl proposition that's got me fighting my head. I just don't know what the hell to make of it."

"That is mighty serious," agreed Morgan. "You can't find a single trace of her, Brood?"

"Not one single bit of sign. According to Jaeger and Cutts she left the J Bar C first thing Tuesday morning, saying she was going to stay at the hotel in town. But she never showed up in town at all. Somewhere between town and the J Bar C she just vanished into thin air."

"How did the word get out?"

"Leek Jaeger came into town Wednesday with the idea of having another talk with her about the Wineglass. I guess you knew that she was Ben Sloan's heir. Well, Jaeger asked for her at the hotel and Joe Lester thought he was crazy. Jaeger insisted that she'd left the J Bar C Tuesday morning, saying she was going to stay at the hotel until she'd made up her mind whether to sell the Wineglass or operate it. Joe Lester swore she was nowhere nigh the hotel and on checking up around town, Jaeger couldn't find a single soul who'd laid eyes on her. He came and told me about it. I been ramming up and down, back and forth, ever since. I've had posse men riding in every direction trying to find some sign. But there ain't a single thing we've been able to locate. She's just gone — that's all."

"That's bad," said Bill Morgan — "plenty bad. In this country we don't mistreat women. Somebody will get their neck stretched for this."

"You're telling me!" exploded Shotwell. "Listen, Morgan — in running my office I try to play the game as impersonal as I can. It is the only way a sheriff can run his job and not run into a peck of misery. I don't show sympathies one way or the other. But I don't mind telling the world right now that I'm just another man who's madder than hell. If I can get my hands on the pole-cat who ran off with that nice girl, I'll forget all about the star I pack and just take him to pieces with my bare hands. So far, I been trying my best to pick up Buck Comstock's trail. But Comstock can run around plumb loose for all of me — until I've found that girl. There's been some talk made —."

Shotwell broke off, as though reluctant to say what had been at the tip of his tongue, but Bill Morgan gave him no chance. "Go on, Brood. What is this talk?"

"Well," grunted Shotwell — "some folks are hinting that maybe it was Comstock who met up with her and packed her off."

It was Bill Morgan's turn to explode. "I want somebody to make that crack to me," he roared. "By Gawd — I do. I'll drive their lying words right back through their teeth with a .45 slug. Don't tell me you're big enough fool to believe anything like that."

"I'm not," said Shotwell. "I slapped one jigger down already, for telling me that was exactly what must have happened."

"Who was that hombre?"

"Duke Younger. I'm not exactly soft in the head about Buck Comstock, after the fool he made of me in his getaway. But I've seen too many men be shoved all the way to hell because people blamed them for everything that had happened, after they had once gotten at outs with the law over one deal. Buck Comstock might be a smoke roller, but he shore ain't the sort to ever harm any woman."

"Brood," said Morgan — "there's been two or three times since you first arrested Buck Comstock when I was ready to brand you as a maverick. I'm apologizing for the thought."

Shotwell laughed harshly. "Being a sheriff is a long way from rump meat and gravy, Bill. Plenty of times a sheriff has to do things he ain't noway crazy about doing. I'm human, same as anybody else, with my own likes and dislikes. There's some folks who will try and tell you different, though. Just the same, give me the benefit of the doubt and you won't be wrong. Well, as long as you can't help me about that girl, I'll be dragging on. If I only could figure out someplace to start. I tell you, Bill — never in all my experience have I been so damned helpless. Most generally a fellow has a few signs to work from. In this case there isn't a damned one."

"I'll pass the word to my crew, Brood," promised Morgan. "I'll keep 'em riding and looking. I'll do the same thing myself. And should anything turn up at all, I'll see that you're notified, pronto. You see, I want to be in on the party myself, for I want to help pull on the rope that hangs the skunk who run off with her."

"Thanks, Bill. That's fair enough. And I'll see there's a place reserved for you on that rope." He smiled, nodded his good-bye, and left.

Sounded the tramp of spurred heels, moving out to the front of the house.

Shortly after, came the muffled tattoo of hoofs, vanishing out toward the west. And when Bill Morgan and Bones Baker returned to the room where Bill had talked with Brood Shotwell, they froze in amazement. There, sitting in a chair and pulling on his boots, was Buck Comstock.

Bones stuttered. "Wh— where in hell did you come from?"

Buck jerked his head. "In there. I heard what Shotwell had to say about the disappearance of Miss Harper. Bill, why the devil didn't you go into town Tuesday, like I told you to? Then you'd have found she hadn't showed up and whoever did run off with her, wouldn't have had a day's start."

Buck was bleak of eye, his face grim and forbidding.

"I did go in, Buck," replied Morgan quietly. "I spent all of Tuesday morning in town, waiting for her to show up. When she didn't show, I figured maybe she'd changed her mind about leaving the J Bar C — at least, about leaving it right away. I came home then, never dreaming that the reason she did not show in town was because she couldn't."

"Sorry, Bill," Buck growled. "Only — that news — about Miss Harper, sort of knocked me for a loop. That's bad, Bill —

147

mighty bad. Her disappearance, I mean. As I see it, there is only one answer."

"You mean — Jaeger and Cutts?"

"No other. I can't see any other answer. This is still pretty wild country, Bill — but good Lord, it ain't so damn wild that a respectable girl can't ride along a well traveled trail close in to town without being run off with by some tough hombre. Shore, I know that Toad Black turned animal, but the set-up was different there. He thought that just he and she were alone out at a ranch, miles from anywhere. But just riding between the J Bar C and town — hell, even a maniac wouldn't have dared bother her there.

"No, this points right at those two buzzards, Cutts and Jaeger. She might have told them that if they wanted the Wineglass they'd have to jump their price, plenty. Or she might have even told them that she didn't care to sell at all — that she intended to keep the spread and run it. Rather than lose their chance of getting the spread, I wouldn't put it past those two to lock her up somewhere and try and force her to sign the Wineglass over to them."

"I can see the possibility of that, all right," nodded Bill Morgan. "What do you suggest?"

"It shapes up this way for me. So far, we been waiting for Jaeger and Cutts to make the first break. We've been set to sort of counter punch, you might say. It ain't getting us anywhere. Jaeger and Cutts are going places while we just stand around fighting our heads. What do you say we walk in on them — swinging?"

Morgan frowned thoughtfully. "It's a heavy decision to make — one that's liable to throw the range into a bloody war, kid. But — if you can pick out a decent angle of attack, I'm with you."

"Good. Bones — you still got Toad Black?"

"Y-betcha," nodded Bones. "I got him — and I'll keep him as long as you want him, Buck. He made one try to break loose and I whammed him over the coco with a frying pan. It shore civilized him, calmed him right down so he's meek as a day-old lamb, right now. Shucks! He gets down on his knees and starts praying when he sees old Bones coming down into the spud cellar."

"You hang on to him, Bones — no matter what comes. Bill, you and I are heading for town."

"Now?"

"Now. Duke Younger will be hanging

around there most likely, lapping up liquor. I want him. I'm going to get him. And then I'm going to make him and Toad Black talk — talk plenty. If I have to, I'll burn the truth out of those two coyotes with hot branding irons. I'm tired of dodging and ducking and hiding out. Long as it was only myself to consider I didn't mind it too much. But now those damned rats are fighting Jean Harper and I'm going to get into things, plumb up to my neck. I'm not going to sit back and let time tell the story. I'm going to jam the truth right out into the open. Coming with me, Bill?"

In answer, Bill Morgan lifted his gun-belts down from a wall peg and buckled them on. He put on his hat and started for the door.

"I'll meet you on the trail, Bill," said Buck. "I got to put my boots on and get my bronc."

It was nine o'clock when Buck Comstock and Bill Morgan rode up to the outskirts of Twin Buttes. They reined in, just short of town.

"You ease around and leave your bronc out back of the hotel, Buck," said Morgan. "I'll go straight in and try and locate Younger. When I've found him I'll meet you in the alley between the hotel and Pete

Allen's store. Then we can figure how to toll Younger far enough out into the shadows so we can throw a gun on him and make him come along peaceable."

Buck reined away through the darkness, circling carefully, alert and watchful. He was taking a long gamble in coming into Twin Buttes like this. Almost anywhere he might run into someone who would recognize him and send up the alarm. Buck had no illusions about the make-up of the average human. They liked to appear in sympathy with the strong side — to align themselves with a winner. Right now, to those who did not know the inside of things, Jaeger and Cutts appeared to be riding high, wide and handsome. Many men would flock to their standard, if for no other reason than to make sure of immunity from the wrath and apparent power of the J Bar C. Those friends whom Buck did possess would go all the way for him, but there were plenty of sycophants running loose who would betray him to Jaeger and Cutts without the least hesitation. Therefore he moved carefully, and surely, alert as some hunted thing.

He reached the back of the hotel however, with all quiet and serene. Here, where the shadows were blackest, he left his

151

horse, then stole on foot up the alley between the hotel and the store. There, a few yards back from the street, he squatted on his heels to wait.

Bill Morgan had no trouble at all in locating Duke Younger. The very first place Morgan looked in — the Yellow Horse Saloon — showed him his man. Younger was standing at the far end of the bar. Drinking with him were Leek Jaeger and another rider who was a stranger to Morgan. This third man was of average height, compact and wiry of build. A long, livid scar ran across the left side of his face, reminder of a wound which must have dug deep enough to shatter the bones of his jaw. For the lower half of his face was queerly drawn and puckered, giving a pointed, rodent expression to his mouth. When he spoke, his words carried a strange, whistling sibilance. He was dressed in average range togs, but he carried two big guns, slung low and tied down. Something in the way he stood and moved, told Morgan the story. Here was a gun man, if he had ever seen one.

Morgan edged up to the bar, spoke or nodded to various acquaintances, ordered and downed a short whiskey. He let his eyes play along the bar and saw that Jaeger and his two companions were looking at him. Jaeger called along the bar in affected friendliness. "Come and have another on me, Bill. And I want you to meet a friend of mine."

Morgan's hesitation was only mental. Jaeger's show of friendliness was only a mask for something else. He'd find out what was behind those little lead colored eyes of Jaeger. He elbowed his way over to the three. "Four whiskies," Jaeger called to the bartender. "Bill — meet Whistler Hahn. I reckon you've heard of him. He's going to work for the J Bar C. Whistler, shake hands with Bill Morgan."

Bill Morgan had heard of Whistler Hahn all right. Few men in that section of the country hadn't. Whistler Hahn was living proof of the old, old adage that a bad reputation always traveled faster and farther than a good one. Whistler Hahn's reputation was enough to curl the hair of the average bad man. And there had been just a trace of emphasis in Jaeger's tone when he said that he had hired Hahn to work for the J Bar C. Bill Morgan missed none of that, either. But his face remained utterly emotionless as he stuck out his hand. "Glad to know you, Hahn."

They downed their drinks. "What do

you think about the disappearance of Miss Harper, Bill?" asked Jaeger.

"Damned if I know what to think," Morgan rumbled. "Brood Shotwell was out to talk that little matter over with me. Brood says he's getting spooked, the way things are going. I'm beginning to feel that way myself. Here Toad Black drops off the face of the earth apparently. And now this Harper girl turns up missing. It's got me fighting my head, for a fact. At the same time, I rise to remark that I can't understand why any man would be low enough to run off with a girl — a nice girl like she seemed to be."

Duke Younger smirked crudely. "Me, I only saw her once — and that was across the courtroom. But I must say, it would be a lot easier to run off with her than a lot of old battle-axes I've seen in my time. She sort of warmed a man's eye, if you ask me."

He brayed with laughter at his own idea of humor. Duke Younger was tall and dark, with high, narrow shoulders. His face was long and horsy, with loose lips and looser chin. His hair was bleached, his eyes pale and evasive.

"She was a right pretty girl, all right," admitted Morgan quietly. "But I still say that any man who would run off with a helpless girl like that, is about fifty degrees lower than a rattlesnake. I can understand men fighting men, but when they start fighting women, they cease to be men and are all yellow coyote. What do you think, Hahn?"

The gunman shrugged, and smiled crookedly. "I been told I got plenty of rough edges — and I reckon I have," he said in that queer, spine chilling, hissing voice which had given rise to his nickname. "But I'm inclined to agree with you, Morgan. Fighting a woman — a good woman, shore is low as hell."

It seemed to the observant Morgan that Leek Jaeger's bull neck was just a trifle redder than usual. And Jaeger switched the subject glibly. "I hear you're building up your crew, Morgan. What's the idea? You ain't figuring on roundup or branding yet, are you?"

"No. But when folks begin to disappear all over the range, a wise man takes note of it and gets ready. Maybe it'll be cattle or horses that'll start to turn up missing next. I aim to be ready for all emergencies, that's all."

"Not such a had idea," admitted Jaeger smoothly. "Incidentally, if you can use still another man, here's a good one." He jerked his head at Duke Younger. "Duke just hit me up for a job, but I told him I was full up. When you came in the thought struck me that maybe you could use him."

"That's the ticket, Bill," said Younger. "How about it? I can't live on my income forever."

Bill Morgan's eyes were veiled and shrewd. He even smiled a little to himself, deep where no one could see it. "I might use you at that, Duke," he said. "I came into town tonight to see Charley Fournier, who had kind of half promised he'd sign on with me. If he does, I'll be full up. If he doesn't, you can have the job, Duke. Stay here for a while. I'll run down Charley and get a final answer from him. Then I'll let you know."

"I'll be waiting right here for you, Bill," promised Younger. "Any kind of a little old job at all will look like a million dollars to me now. I'm broke flatter than a postage stamp. If I get the job, better be prepared to shuck out a little advance for me. I'll need it to buy smoking." Again he brayed with laughter.

When Bill Morgan left the Yellow Horse, his eyes had sharpened to disgust and fury. "The damned slick polecat," he muttered.

"Does he think he's fooling me any? Well, he's not — not by a jugful. I see his little idea all right, all right."

Bill went down the street to the far end, cut across and came back to Pete Allen's store. He went in, killed a few minutes talking to Pete, then came out to pause and build a cigarette, his deep set eyes busy up and down the street. Seeing that all was clear, he took a few quick strides and ducked into the alley between the store and the hotel.

"Any luck, Bill?" came Buck Comstock's voice.

"Best in the world," snapped Morgan. "Younger is over in the Yellow Horse with Jaeger and Whistler Hahn. They —."

"Whistler Hahn!" exclaimed Buck. "Not THE Whistler Hahn?"

"Nobody else but him, Buck. It's Hahn, the gunfighter all right. And he's going to work for Jaeger. Jaeger told me that himself. But I got to make this quick. Jaeger asked me why I was increasing my crew and I told him straight out that I didn't like the way things were shaping up on this range. Then he suggested that I hire Younger, if I needed another man. I told them I was dickering with Charley Fournier about a job, but if Charley couldn't get away to work for me, I'd take on Younger. I'm supposed to be talking it over with Fournier, now. Younger said he'd wait in the Yellow Horse until I got back. Buck, does it tell anything to you?"

"Plenty," was the terse reply. "Younger is Jaeger's man — always has been. What Jaeger is after is to get a spy in our camp, Bill. He's trying this trick to get one. He wants Younger in our crowd. You're hiring Younger, of course?"

"Sure," admitted Morgan, with a grim chuckle. "Hiring him just long enough to get him out to the ranch, where I'll jam a gun in his ribs and send him to help Toad Black hold down the spud cellar."

"That's the stuff, Bill. I'll be out at the Circle Star waiting for you. So Jaeger and Cutts have brought in Whistler Hahn, eh? Well, the tide is building up, Bill. One of these days the dam is going to bust wide open and there'll be hell and sudden death spread all over this range. Okay, Bill — you go get Younger and I'll drift out to the ranch. See you later."

Bill Morgan took another careful survey of the street, ducked out of the alley and headed leisurely for the Yellow Horse. Buck slid cautiously back along the alley and out into the open behind the hotel. He crossed to where he had left his bronco, dimly sensing the bulk of the animal. He picked up the reins, threaded them about the animal's neck and reached for the stirrup. There was the faintest of sounds behind him and then a hard object was jammed against his spine. A cold voice reached him, the voice of Sheriff Brood Shotwell.

"Too bad, Buck — but reach high! You shouldn't have been fool enough to come this close to town. Get 'em up!"

CHAPTER SEVEN

As a captive, hands and feet tied, head and face muffled in a blanket, Jean Harper had little idea where that long, long ride through the night took her. There were innumerable turnings and twistings, which, if intended to muddle her, so that she would have no idea of her ultimate destination, were entirely unnecessary. Even an Indian would have been thoroughly and hopelessly confused if carried off under the same conditions. And Jean was no Indian. She was a slim, scared stripling of a girl, doing her best to fight down the threads of panic which kept rising in her, and to keep a clear head and reasonable courage to face this thing through, whatever it might be and wherever it might lead.

Before long her aching wrists and ankles became numb and heavy from stricture. Unable to use the stirrups because of the way her ankles were tied to the cinch rings, the rack and lurch of the horse punished her. Her shoulders were cramped, her back ached. This discomfort did not daunt her. It served the purpose of keeping her anger kindled, and with anger came defiance and courage. If these two renegades thought that they could bluff or bulldoze a lone, helpless girl, they were badly mistaken. Jean's determination was thoroughly set on one thing. Cutts and Jaeger would never, never get their dirty, greedy paws on the Wineglass ranch now, no matter what they did, or how much money they might offer her.

Another thought came to her, and with it a quick, truant thrill of warmth. She believed Buck Comstock's story now without any reservations whatsoever. For if Jaeger and Cutts would use such tactics as these in their effort to force her to sell them her ranch at their own figure, they were more than capable of trying to railroad an enemy who was standing in their way.

The ride came to an end at last. The horses were pulled to a halt. Cutts spoke. "I'll go on ahead, Leek. There might be some objection. I can wield the verbal whip better than you can. And even if he does kick, I pack enough guns to make him knuckle under. I'll be back as soon as I can."

There came a period of considerable

wait. Somewhere in the far distance a coyote wailed to the stars. The horses shifted and stamped restlessly about with Leek Jaeger, from time to time, quieting them with harsh tones.

Jean could tell that Jaeger was uneasy. No doubt the man was thinking now, thinking of the retribution which would come his way if some stray cowpuncher or two should happen upon them. For though Jean had been in this western country but a comparatively short time she had judged the majority of the wild riding cowboys to be men who would go fighting mad over the mistreatment of a woman. How fresh in her memory were the actions of Buck Comstock over this same thing. And if he, a fugitive from law would chance all he did to come to her aid — what would be the reactions of riders not on the dodge should they stumble upon her and Jaeger at this moment? Jean could only imagine it. Yes, Jaeger had plenty to be worried about.

In the end, Cutts came back. "Everything is set," he exclaimed exultantly. "And there is just the set-up we want. We'll leave the horses here. Help me get her off."

Ankles freed once more, Jean was lifted to the ground. But her feet felt dead from stricture and she would have fallen if the two men had not supported her on either side. Half carried, half dragged, Jean was taken forward. A low voice hailed them in a crusty, whining voice. Cutts answered.

Abruptly Jean realized they were close to a house. Strange how one could sense a thing of that sort. There had been no sound of any sort which would have suggested a dwelling, but Jean knew it, just the same. The irrelevant thought struck her that even a house had a personality, perhaps.

Her fumbling feet stumbled over a threshold. Board floor was under her now. There was a roof over her. Two more doorways were crowded through. Then Jean's knees struck the edge of a bunk. She was pushed down upon it. A door closed behind her.

"I'm going to free you and take that blanket away," said Frank Cutts. "But see that you behave yourself. It won't do you the slightest good to struggle or scream. There's no one to hear — or care."

The blanket was lifted away and in another moment her wrists were freed. Jean lay as she was on the bunk, looking around her. She was in a room not over ten feet square, barren and empty except for the bunk on which she lay, and a couple of old, rawhide backed chairs. An empty box in one corner supported a small kerosene lamp, the light of which filled the room with a garish, feeble light.

Leek Jaeger was standing with his back against the closed door. Frank Cutts stood beside the bunk. He smiled, only with his eyes and then without the slightest mirth. Cold purpose and rampant cruelty was in that smile.

"I know," he drawled mockingly — "that you haven't the slightest idea where you are, Miss Harper. That is as it should be of course, from the viewpoint of Leek and myself. But there is one thing I can tell you. Here you stay until you decide that you are willing to listen to reason."

Jean lifted herself on one elbow. Her dark eyes flayed both of the rascals with scorn — her red lips curled with it. "If," she flamed, "by reason you mean that I listen favorably to the offer of you two scoundrels to buy, or steal my ranch — then I'll be in this room the rest of my life. No matter how I might have felt about the matter before, now I am absolutely certain of one thing. You'll never, never, *never* get your crooked hands on my ranch. What a fine pair of cowardly, lying, underhanded curs you are!"

This outburst rather startled the two men. It was plain that they expected to have by this time only a frightened, cowering girl to deal with, a slim terrified youngster who would be only too glad to bargain for her freedom. Instead, they stood quailing under the scorn and utter contempt of a regular little tiger cat.

Leek Jaeger would not meet her eyes, but stood looking here and there, shifting uneasily about on clumsy feet. Cutts was the first of the two to recover, and for the first time the cold mask slipped completely from his face, leaving it convulsed in a savage spasm of anger. And right then Jean Harper knew that of the two men, Frank Cutts — immaculate dresser and ex-gambler — was by far the most dangerous to deal with.

"All right," he grated harshly. "Have your say, you little fool. We'll let you cool your heels for a while in here. If that doesn't bring you to your senses, we'll try other — and sterner methods. Think, think hard. You'll come to the realization that you have a lot more to lose than gain by acting stubborn. Pin this one fact in your hat — we're going to get control of the Wineglass, if you have to disappear permanent and for all time. Acting the proud and haughty lady isn't going to do you the slightest good. I've handled stubborn women before. There are always ways and means of bringing them to time. All right, Leek — take that lamp."

They backed out of the door and closed it behind them, leaving Jean in utter, stygian blackness. She heard the click of a padlock. Steps moved away. Silence settled in. And then, and only then, did Jean turn face downward on the blankets, bury her head in her arms and give way to her feelings. After all there was a limit to her self-control.

Half an hour later she sat up, mopped her eyes dry with the backs of her hands. Those tears had done her a lot of good. Her head was strangely clear. She settled back for a period of clear, common sense thought. There was no use in being stampeded by this set-up. She knew exactly the purpose behind this abduction. Badly as Jaeger and Cutts wanted the Wineglass they could never get it as long as she refused to sell it to them, or sign it over for any other consideration.

It was inevitable that her absence from the J Bar C would be discovered and that Jaeger and Cutts would be called on for explanation. They'd lie, of course — for the truth wasn't in either of them. But no matter what their answer might be, men would begin looking for her. Sooner or later, someone would get a trace of her. It was all a matter of time. There was only one thing to do and that was to be philosophical about it. For the time she was safe enough. Jaeger and Cutts could run their bluff only so far.

She got up and moved about the room, feeling her way. Just four walls — and not very spacious ones, either. In one of them was a window, with the glass broken from the sash in several places. Exploring fingers told Jean that this window had been solidly boarded up from the outside, though the cracks between the boards were wide enough to let in the cool, moist breath of the night. She stood there by the window for a time, letting those currents of sweet air play over her face and throat. In the distance she heard a cow bawl plaintively.

Obviously her prison was a ranchhouse of some kind, but just which one it was, or where it might be, Jean had not the slightest idea. A sudden thought struck her. Maybe she was still at the J Bar C. Maybe Cutts and Jaeger had taken her on that long ride through the night, with all those twistings and turnings to confuse her, and then brought her back to the J Bar C to lock her up. She immediately discarded that thought, however. If Cutts and Jaeger had wanted to keep her at the J Bar C they would never have bothered to take her out of it in the first place. They would have, as soon as they first overpowered her, lugged her off and locked her up in some part of the house. No, this wasn't the J Bar C. It was some other ranch.

Maybe it was the Wineglass! Maybe at this very moment she was locked in her own ranchhouse! She left the window and felt her way to the door. She threw all her weight against it several times, but her only reward for this effort was a bruised shoulder on her part and a slight creaking as the door stood solid and unmovable. Escape, by way of that door, was out of the question.

She went back to the bunk and stretched out upon it, staring with wide eyes at the invisible ceiling above. Lying there so still, her nostrils picked up a scent strangely reminiscent of the old grocery store, to which many times when a little girl, she had run errands for her mother. It was the scent of bacon and dried onions — of flour and coffee and dried fruit. Her prison had evidently, at one time, been a storeroom for provisions.

She brought her mind back to sober realities. After all, how much chance of rescue did she really have? She had to admit that there existed very little at all in the immediate present. Jaeger and Cutts were just cunning enough to cover their tracks pretty well. They were smooth, those two — smooth and tricky.

Considering the possibility of rescue, it was not strange that at this moment, the figure of Buck Comstock should sweep again into her consciousness. He it was who had rescued her before. Perhaps Fate had ordained that he would play that same role again. In a way it was ridiculous to play with such a thought. Buck Comstock was hiding out, a fugitive from law. Even if he should in some manner learn of her whereabouts, what could he do toward a rescue? He was only one lone man and, terrific and dauntless fighter though he might be, there were limits to what any one man could do. For that matter, why should he bother to take any more risks for her sake? The two of them were still, to all practical intents and purposes, virtual strangers. And Buck Comstock had his own problems to worry about.

Yet — what was that he had said to her — as he held her hand in goodbye? "Not goodbye. Rather — hasta la vista. Until we meet again." Her cheeks warmed hotly, in the darkness. That lean, sun-blackened cowboy — with his mobile lips and direct, keen eyes —.

A forlorn loneliness descended upon her. Everything was so still — and she was so much alone. It took a real effort to keep away from the tears again. It was better, she decided, not to think at all. Thoughts built hopes and these hopes, put under the searching light of plain practical reasoning, fell drearily apart. And that made her want to cry. She relaxed, pulled a blanket over her and searched for sleep. Emotionally and physically spent, sleep took her all of a sudden. She was a little restless in that sleep. Once or twice she moaned a trifle, like an infant plagued with dreams.

She awoke to the realization that some-one was in the room with her. A vague half-light permeated her prison. Against the cracks of the boards over the window the bright gold of sunlight lay. Another day was at hand.

Frank Cutts stood over her. There were dishes on one of the chairs. The rich, heart-ening aroma of fresh coffee filled the air. "Your breakfast," said Cutts as he saw her eyes open. "I'll talk to you while you eat."

Jean, her long, black, curved lashes lifting sleepily, surprised an expression in the glance of Cutts which made her flesh creep and her veins run with ice water. It was as though some evil satyr had been leering and smirking at her while she slept. This man would be capable of incredible evil. Incipient panic stirred in her breast, but she fought it back heroically.

Despite her uneasiness and smothered terror, she was hungry enough. Her slender body was too vigorous and sturdy not to call for sustenance. She threw aside the blanket, got to her feet, stifling a yawn. She glanced at the lines of golden sunlight which pierced the boarded window and immediately felt better. Outside it was day — and the clean warm sun was shining. Her courage came back to her.

"I haven't the slightest desire to talk with you, Mr. Cutts," she told him coolly. "There is nothing you could say that would be of the slightest interest to me. I would not believe you, no matter what you told me or promised. And considering the Wineglass ranch, the matter is a closed subject, as far as I am concerned. I'll enjoy my breakfast so much more if you'll leave me to myself."

Again the cold mask of Cutts's face slid

aside. He caught at her arm, but she dodged away from him. "You'll listen to me and you'll talk to me, and you'll do as I ask — or wish you had," he gritted. "Once and for all get it out of your head that I'm bluffing. I'm too old a hand at the game not to know when to quit bluffing and get down to cold cases."

Jean did not even appear to hear him. She drew up the other chair and began to eat hungrily. She ignored Cutts entirely. But he refused to be ignored. "Get all this," he snarled. "If you know what is good for you, you'll do business with Leek Jaeger and me. I told you last night that we want the Wineglass range. I told you that we intend to get it — no matter what the means used — nor the cost entailed. One way or another we get it. You've got just this one more chance to get out of this affair with some money in your pocket — and the right to look other people in the eye. I think you know what I mean."

Jean's eyes were devastating as they flamed at him. "You contemptible rat!"

Cutts laughed harshly, then. "You remember the offer Jaeger and I made you, last night. Seventy-five hundred. Our final offer — and not one cent more."

"And you remember my answer," Jean

retorted. "You'll not get that ranch, not even if you offered seven million. And now I want to tell you one more thing, Mister Frank Cutts. I haven't been out on this range country very long, but there are a few things that I've figured out. One is that my disappearance is bound to be noted, sooner or later. Men will search. In the end they will find me and I will tell them everything. And no matter what has happened to me, I know what the temper of those men will be. You and your fellow rat — Leek Jaeger — will be hung!"

Cutts stood very still. Jean did not know it, but those words hit Frank Cutts at the very weakest chink in his armor of frozen-faced impassivity. Once, years before, Cutts had seen a man lynched. He had never forgotten that picture. It had been graven on the retina of his mind so deeply and stayed with him with such maddening constancy that at times he felt it to be prophetic of his own end. The horror of that thought had become a veritable mania with him.

Jean was too busy with her food to notice the tiny beads of cold sweat which grew on the renegade gambler's forehead, or to note the deepening pallor which swept over his face. He began to pace up and down the room, jerkily, explosively. He fought to put aside that mental nightmare conjured up by the girl's chance remark.

It came to him that he was far too deep in this thing now, to weaken in any way. For even if he were to turn this girl loose right now, the relentless wrath of the whole surrounding range would descend upon him and that rope — that rope which haunted him, would be reaching out its noose for him. He could see that his only hope of success lay in going forward with absolute ruthlessness. If he could demean this girl, shame her, break her spirit, force her to accede to his demands — then he might, under the cover of darkness, smuggle her far, far away — clear across the Border, if necessary and there make arrangements to see that she never returned. He had to crush her, utterly — he could realize that, now.

He stopped his pacing, turned and looked at her and the curtains were completely stripped from his savage eyes now and his purpose lay stark and ugly in them.

Jean, her head tipped back as she drained her coffeecup, saw that purpose and recognized it. In a flash she was on her feet. As he lunged for her she hurled that heavy coffee mug with all her strength. It crashed to bits, high up on his head, staggering him and bringing a fan of blood down across his forehead.

Jean leaped for the door, then, but he had her before she could reach it. She opened her mouth to scream and he clamped a palm brutally across her lips. His other arm wound about her with crushing force.

She fought wildly with an amazing display of desperate strength. They staggered up and down the room, knocking over first one chair and then the other, sending dishes cascading to the floor. They slipped and stumbled over those dishes, crushing some of them underfoot. Cutts was panting feral, blistering curses. They crashed against the wall, against the door.

That first mad burst of strength on Jean's part was soon dissipated. She was no match for this savage brute who held her. Panic rose in her until she thought her swelling throat would burst. Terror, despair clogged her mind. If she could only get her lips free long enough to scream! Like a frantic little animal she set her white teeth in Cutts' palm and bit deep.

A hard, rasping cough of fury and pain broke from the throat of Cutts and he jerked the wounded hand away. And before Jean could make a sound he clubbed her brutally with a clenched fist. Deadening agony flooded her head on the heels of that blow. Her senses began to slip. And when Cutts threw her to one side she fell limply half on the bunk, half on the floor. At that moment the door of the room opened.

Jean was too near unconsciousness to know who was there or even to look. But dimly she heard a thin, nasal voice speaking. "That'll be all of that kind of business, Cutts. No, don't make a move for your gun or I'll blow your heart out. I told you last night, when you brought her here that she'd be treated like a lady. I know I got to crawl to you — but I crawl just so far. This kind of thing is out. You better leave, now. And the next time you come into this room, I come along. I still got a little man left in me."

Cutts said no word as he walked out. The door slammed shut and a lock clicked. Moaning and shuddering, Jean crept to the bunk and fainted.

CHAPTER EIGHT

It seemed to Buck Comstock, as he felt the double impact of Sheriff Brood Shotwell's voice in his ears and gun against his spine, that a complete panorama of life spread itself before the eye of his memory. He saw it all, the hard work, the danger and hardship. He saw its triumphs and moments of despair, its highlights and drab shadows. He saw what he had been through in this present crisis, what freedom meant to himself and to his friends. And he saw what his future would be — behind the walls of Pinole.

Buck dropped the reins and let go of the stirrup. His hands began to lift. "All right, Brood," he said wearily. "You got me."

And then he was whirling, leaping — and his right hand lashed out and down. It was the most desperate chance he had ever taken in his life. For no intelligent reason, it worked. That clawing right hand smashed full upon Shotwell's gun, locked the spurred hammer back. With the same move his left forearm blocked out, striking the sheriff across the throat like a bar of iron. And Buck's left foot was driving in and lifting, cutting Shotwell's feet from under him.

They went down together, heavily — with Buck on top. That smashing fall to the ground seemed to half stun the sheriff and Buck twisted the gun from Shotwell's weakening grip. And then Buck, reversing the gun, jammed the deadly muzzle against Shotwell's side.

"Quiet!" he hissed. "Quiet, Brood. I'm sorry that I had to pull this. But I'm not going to Pinole, Brood. You'll have to bury me first."

Shotwell gagged and choked a bit from the effects of that fall and from the blow across his throat from Buck's forearm. When he did speak his voice was quiet and even.

"You're only making things worse for yourself, Buck. You can't keep away from me forever."

"I'm going to try," snapped Buck harshly. "Damn it, man — why did you have to come along now? I got nothing against you personally, Brood. I don't want to hurt you in any way, for you and I used to be pretty good friends before all this trouble started. Yet, if I don't keep you quiet someway, I won't be ten feet from town before you'll have the alarm out. And I can't afford to be jagging all over hell tonight with a posse at my heels. I got important business to tend to."

"That," said Shotwell, with a thin, mirthless chuckle — "that is your problem to figure out, Buck."

Buck scowled down at the sheriff. What the devil could he do with this man, now he had him? He himself had to get out to the Circle Star as soon as possible. Bill Morgan would be heading that way with Duke Younger. So awful much depended on what turned up, this night. It looked like he'd have to gag and tie Shotwell and hide him some place. And then, in his dilemma, a thought came to Buck, a thought which brought him crouching even lower and which put a vibrant eagerness into his voice.

"Listen, Brood — when you were out at the Circle S, early this evening talking to Bill Morgan about the disappearance of Toad Black and of that girl, Jean Harper, I was in the next room, listening. No, Bill didn't know I was there. I'd sneaked into the house by an open window, and when I showed myself after you had gone, Bill was plenty surprised. But I heard all you said.

"You know, Brood — there's been several times, particularly during the past month or two when I began to doubt your make-up. I was getting to the point where I felt you were just about as crooked as all the rest of 'em. But by what you said to Bill Morgan tonight, and you were speaking your plain, true thoughts, I decided different. I think, deep down, you're square, Brood. I'm going to gamble that way. I want you to ride out to the Circle Star with me — now. There's going to be some strange things said out there, and I want a bonafide witness to hear those things said. If I'm seeing things straight, you'll get an earful, Brood — one that'll make you sit up plenty straight. After you've heard all there is to be heard, I'm going to leave it up to you. If you still want to bring me in — then I'll come quiet and you can pack me off to Pinole and lock me up for good. How about it?"

For a long moment Shotwell was silent. "That," he said slowly — "that don't make sense. What is all this I'm expected to listen to?"

"You'll have to wait until we get out to the ranch for that," said Buck. "It won't be me who'll be telling all the things I want

180

you to hear. You'll be surprised, Brood — plenty surprised."

"And you'll leave it up to me?" murmured the sheriff. "You won't put up a fight if I decide to bring you back to town? You give me your word on that, Buck?"

"I'll give you my word, Brood."

"It still don't make sense," said Shotwell. "But your word is good with me, Buck. I'll go with you."

Buck caught him by the shoulder, lifted him to his feet. "Here's your gun, Brood," he said simply. "Go get a bronc. I'll meet you on the trail."

Slowly Shotwell holstered his weapon. He was staring queerly at Buck through the darkness. He nodded. "I'll meet you," he said.

Shotwell found Buck waiting for him along the trail less than a hundred yards from town. Without a word they swung into it, side by side, pounding swiftly along across Timber Valley, up and over the sage tableland beyond and down finally into Coyote Valley and on to the Circle Star ranchhouse.

"This," said Shotwell, as they dismounted at the corrals, "is the damnedest fool thing I ever did in my life, Buck Comstock. I hope you're not going to make a fool of me."

Buck laughed shortly. "Not a chance, Brood. Try and get my viewpoint. Things lay both ways for me. I got such a hell of a lot to win and everything, even my life, to lose. I ain't liable to be leading you on any fairy story chase, am I?"

"No," agreed Shotwell. "I reckon you know what you're doing, Buck."

Bones Baker answered Buck's knock and stared in bug-eyed, wordless amazement as Buck and Shotwell walked into the ranch-house. Bones saw that both Shotwell and Buck wore guns. Here were sheriff and fugitive, side by side in apparent friendliness with no quarrel between them at all that Bones could see. The fat cook began to stutter.

"Wh— what the — how the — say, just what in heh— heh— hell — ?"

Buck grinned briefly at Bones' loss for words and the look on his face. "Whistle," he advised cheerfully. "Whistle, Bones — before you explode. Big doings tonight. You still got Toad Black in safe keeping?"

"Yuh, yup," stammered Bones. "I got him."

"Toad Black!" Shotwell whirled and stared at Buck.

Buck laughed. "That's right, Brood. He's here. I'll produce him in a minute. He's one of the two hombres who's going to say

182

a lot of the things I brought you out here to listen to. Think hard, Brood — and maybe you'll begin to get the drift."

Shotwell thought hard, grunted. "Who's the other hombre you speak of?"

"Duke Younger." Buck went to the outer door, listened a moment, then nodded. "Bill and Younger will be here in a minute. I can hear their broncs. Brood, you go in that room and shut the door. I may have to act up pretty rough. I don't particularly care for the chore, but it means liberty and a clean name for me. So don't you interfere, Brood — even if it sounds like the house is coming down. And don't you show yourself until I call you. All I want you to do is listen. All right. I hear Bill and Younger outside."

Brood Shotwell, face frowning and thoughtful, went into the other room and shut the door. And not two minutes later Duke Younger walked into the room, his steps laggard and uncertain. There was a wild, scared look about Younger. He had his hands in the air and his gun was gone. Bill Morgan, drawn gun jammed against Younger's back, was herding the fellow unceremoniously along.

At sight of Buck, Duke Younger seemed to wilt. Bill Morgan kicked a chair into place just in time to catch Younger as the fellow's knees seemed to give away.

"Stay put, and not a move or word out of you until you're told to speak, Younger," ordered Morgan sternly. "Else it will be your hard luck." Younger sat down and clasped sweating hands on his knees.

Buck took off his guns and handed them to Bill Morgan. "Take care of these, Bill. Bones, you shut and lock that outer door — then bring Toad Black in here."

Bones, patently bewildered at all these unexpected arrivals, waddled off, snorting through his nose.

At mention of Toad Black, Younger caught his breath in a gasp and began to bluster. "I don't know what all this is about, but you can't treat no white man like this. You can't —."

"Shut up!" growled Bill Morgan, making a jabbing movement with his gun. Younger winced, cringed and subsided, chewing his lips while his eyes darted here and there in desperation.

A moment or two later, shuffling footsteps sounded and Toad Black came in, looking more uncouth and animal-like than the last time Buck had seen him. Black's eyes went straight to Buck and a plain glint of fear showed in them.

"Good enough," drawled Buck. "Bill, you and Bones just listen and look on. Don't interfere. I'll handle this thing. Black," and here his voice took on the crackle of thin ice — "You ready to open up and do some talking?"

Toad Black licked his lips. "Talkin'?" blurted the renegade. "What kind of talkin'? I don't know what you mean."

"Yes you do. I want the truth about that verdict of guilty that the jury brought in against me. Who fixed that jury?"

Black first looked startled, then sulkily stubborn. He shook his head. "I don't know nothin' —."

SMACK!

The sound of Buck's right hand, palm open and flat as it struck Black's face, was like a small report. Black staggered back, feeling of his face, an involuntary curse breaking from his lips. Buck followed him and stood with feet spread, shoulders loose and ready, fists tightening into knots of rawhide.

"You know plenty," Buck lashed. "You know that somebody fixed that jury, gave them instructions to vote me guilty, no matter what the evidence. And you're going to tell us all about it — now! Else the beating I gave you last time will be a picnic to what I'll hand you now. Better believe I mean business, Black. My liberty, my future, my life even — all are at stake. And if you think I'm not going to fight for them, you are crazy. I'll beat you down, I'll butcher you with my bare fists — but by God — you're going to talk."

Buck Comstock seemed to gain in stature as he spoke. The set leanness of his face was so marked, it seemed almost ridged, sharp of angle. His grey eyes held the raw, cold, flawless spark of new cut steel. An air of savage relentlessness settled over him.

Toad Black's bulging, frog-like eyes moved over Buck, pausing but a scant moment on Buck's face, then moving on. He spoke to Bill Morgan. "I'm your prisoner here," he blurted. "You going to stand for this?"

Bill Morgan shrugged. "You're not my prisoner. You're Buck's. He brought you here and I've just been holding you for him. Get me right, Black. Buck is playing his own hand — and I'm backing him, all the way."

Black licked his lips again, heavy lips, lips still puffed and bruised from his last set-to with Buck Comstock. A sudden, hot, stubborn rage flared up in him. "I'll see you in hell before I say a word," he snarled.

Buck weaved in. Toad Black threw his left arm up in a gesture of involuntary defense and clubbed his right at Buck's face. Buck went in under the blow and slashed a savage fist into Black's body. That punch wrung a gasp from the renegade and seemed to touch off in one wild explosion the charge of dammed up dynamite feeling in Buck.

He swarmed all over his man, rocking that bullet head back and forth with ripping, merciless fists, switching his attack to Black's body as the renegade's hands went up to shield his battered face, then going back at Black's face as the body punishment once more dragged the fellow's guard down.

Black had tried a few wild blows, none of which seemed to have the slightest effect on the savage man before him. For the most part he seemed intent on only one thing, and that was to shield himself as best he could from that merciless barrage of punches which rocked him and tore him and beat the blood from him.

Bill Morgan and Bones Baker watched the conflict with cold, measuring eyes. Duke Younger watched it also, but his face grew more pallid and sweating with every blow and his loose mouth began to shake and slaver in fright.

Abruptly Toad Black gave up backing away and charged in — a bull of a man gone berserk under the flailing punishment of flinty fists. Buck, watching his chance, knocked the renegade flat with a right hand blast to the jaw.

Toad Black did not stay down. He came up roaring and Buck knocked him down again with another rapier punch. This time Black arose more slowly and, as Buck glided in on him, set himself and kicked — out and upward, driving a booted foot at Buck in an effort to maim and cripple. That kick would have paralyzed Buck, dropped him cold, had it landed squarely. But Buck was moving to the side as the kick started and took the impact on the thigh of his left leg.

Buck nearly went down, for the blow whirled him completely around and drove him the width of the room, where he came up with a crash against the wall. Black, blubbering an animal cry, charged after him.

Buck's left leg was nearly paralyzed and it rocked and wobbled queerly under him. Yet, somehow, he managed to stagger out of line of Black's rush, where he set himself on his sound leg and smashed Black a blow to the face which rocked him on his heels. Then Buck became a madman. Half hopping, half dragging his left leg, he went after Black in a white fury. His punches became faster, the impact of his fists more crushing.

Black began to wobble and stagger. He gave back and back until a wall stayed any further retreat. And there Buck cut him down in an avalanche of blows. Toad Black's knees buckled and he slid toward the floor. On his knees he wavered for a moment. Then he fell forward on his face, gasping, groaning, twitching.

Buck turned, and his savage, bitter eyes fell on the shrinking, pallid Duke Younger. "You're next," he panted. "I'm not through with that stubborn hog — yet. Soon as he can stand on his feet again, I take up where I left off with him. Between now and then — I work on you, Younger. Get on your feet, you crooked, lying rat."

But Duke Younger did not stand, nor make any move toward standing. Instead, he cowered down in his chair, licking his trembling lips. Buck started across the room toward him, moving more steadily on his feet, now that the paralysis was leaving his left leg.

There was something utterly certain, utterly remorseless in that advance of Buck Comstock — like the steady, onward sweep of a storm cloud, filled with white lightning. Duke Younger cowered lower and lower, and of a sudden went all to pieces.

"No!" he gasped frantically. "No! Don't hit me — don't hit me! I'll talk — I'll talk! That jury was fixed. Every man on it got a hundred dollars — cold cash. I got it — Black got it. We all got it. The jury was fixed, I tell you."

Bill Morgan gave vent to a long sigh, as though a vast relief had come over him. He whirled on Duke Younger and fixed him with a cold, penetrating eye. "Who fixed that jury?" he demanded. "Who gave you that hundred dollars?"

Younger looked around like a trapped animal. He gulped, licked his lips and hesitated. Buck Comstock slithered forward, flinty fists loose and swinging, eyes glittering and implacable. "Better talk, Younger," he gritted. "You'll not be given another chance."

Duke Younger caved. "Jaeger," he gulped hoarsely. "Jaeger and Cutts. They bought that jury — they passed out the money. They told us to vote guilty — no matter what the evidence!"

Buck drew a long breath and turned. Toad Black was up on one elbow, glaring at Younger. Buck stepped over to him. "That correct, Black?" he demanded, his voice silky with menace. "Is Younger telling the truth?"

Toad Black stared up at Buck through eyes filmed and smeared with the punishment he had undergone. Now that old fear came back into them. It was as though he knew that Buck Comstock would always stand over him like this — that no matter what he did, Buck Comstock would always beat him down, drive him to the floor, pound him to a sodden, quivering bulk. He nodded shakily. "Yeah," he croaked thickly. "Younger is right. He's telling you the truth."

Buck went swiftly to the inner door, flung it wide. "All right, Brood," he called. "Come on in."

There was a strange look on Sheriff Brood Shotwell's face as he stepped into the light. A vast, burning contempt flamed in his eyes as he glanced at Toad Black and Duke Younger. His glance moved on to Buck, and he put out his hand.

"Shake, Buck," he said curtly. "I'm sorry I've been part and parcel to such a rotten deal as was put over on you. From the first

I've suspected something along this line, but I had no way of proving it, nor did I imagine it was ever quite as raw as it turns out to be. Whether you want to believe me or not, my intentions were, from the very first, after you were safely in Pinole, to do a lot of investigating on the quiet to try and bring out some proof of the crookedness which my better sense told me was in that trial. I wasn't spreading my intentions for anyone to see. But I had 'em, just the same. And at the same time, I had to make a show of going through with my official duty."

He paused, while a slow, grim smile came over his face. "I might also add that the night you made your first getaway — and tonight, in town — I could have been a little faster and a little harder to handle in all ways, if I had tried real hard. Also, while you been hanging out pretty well back in Big Sage Desert, I could have ridden a long way back into that desert if I'd made my mind up to it."

Buck understood. "I'm apologizing for all the hard thoughts, Brood," he said simply.

"That goes for me, too," murmured Bill Morgan.

"And here," chirruped Bones Baker.

"You can even call me a tub of lard again, Brood — and I won't fight."

Brood Shotwell's smile broadened, but was wiped swiftly away as he looked again at Duke Younger and Toad Black. "Can I have these two rats, Buck?"

"They're all yours, Brood," Buck nodded. "I'm done with them. I got what I wanted out of them. What do you intend doing with those two?"

"First, they go to town, to face Judge Henning, and tell him exactly what they told us — tonight. After that I'm liable to take a quirt and cut my initials in them."

Buck frowned slightly. "Remember what Jaeger told you, Brood — the night I made a break for it from jail? I don't want you to jeopardize your job too much. With election only three months away."

Sheriff Brood Shotwell made a short, fierce gesture. "I've been sheriff in this neck of the woods for a long time, Buck. I like the job — and I'd like to keep it. But if it means — to keep it — that I've got to sell out on square shooting and honesty — I don't want the office. While I wear this star it is going to be kept free of tarnish. I've never smeared it before and I don't intend to start in now. If, three months from now the Twin Buttes range decides it wants a different kind of sheriff than I've been — let it be that way. I'll still be able to live with myself — and I reckon, in this life, that that is the main thing. It must be awful tough on a man to go down into the final shadows, hating himself. All right, you Black — and Younger — get on your feet. We're traveling."

"Miss Harper?" asked Buck. "Have you picked up any line on her yet?"

"No. I'm frank to admit that set-up has got me fighting my head. And I don't know just what to think or where to begin," Shotwell admitted.

"She's got to be somewhere," Buck argued. "She couldn't have just vanished into midair. This is a pretty hardheaded world, Brood. Miracles only happen in fancy. So — why not try searching every ranchhouse on the Twin Buttes range, Brood?"

Shotwell gave Buck a long and searching look. "That," he admitted slowly — "is an idea with possibilities. I was dumb not to think of it before. I think, tomorrow, I'll have to act on that little suggestion. By gollies — I think I will."

"One more thing, Brood. I can circulate as free as I please, now?"

"For all my office will have to say about

it, you shore can, Buck," answered Shotwell quietly. "Yeah, you can come and go as you please. Technically, of course, you should be put in the clear first by due process of law. That will soon be taken care of. When Judge Henning hears what these two polecats have to say, I'll see that he wastes no time giving you lawful clearance. What the hell are you grinning about, Black?"

It was more of a leer on Toad Black's face than a smile. His pulped and swollen features would permit nothing more than a grimace. To Shotwell's terse question he merely shrugged. "You ain't through hearing things," was all Toad Black mumbled.

"It wouldn't surprise me any," rasped the sheriff. "You — Black and Younger — March! Gentlemen — adios!"

Morgan and Bones Baker went out with the sheriff to help tie the prisoners on their horses. Buck lowered himself in the chair Younger had vacated and rubbed his bruised thigh absently. A great peace had come over him. There were other things to be done, of course — and the battle was far from won. But he had gained his primary objective. He was square once more with the law — and that meant with the world. He was free to come and go as he wished, he was in the clear. No more would he have to dodge and hide out and creep around in the dark. It was a good feeling and he relaxed with a little sigh of weariness.

He stared at his bloody fists. He hadn't enjoyed the chore of clubbing Toad Black to reason. There was no satisfaction in personally beating a man who already had two strikes on him, even though that man was as foul a renegade as you'd find in a year of hard travel. Yet it had been a necessary chore, distasteful, but important. And it had gotten results. Weighed by calm judgment, the walloping Black had absorbed did not remotely approach in importance the results it had achieved. Black would get over it and live to absorb a lot more from many men. Yeah, it was a good feeling to know that the threat of the law had been removed.

Bill Morgan and Bones Baker came back. Bones scuttled away and returned with three glasses and a bottle of whiskey. "This calls for a drink, all around," he puffed. "Congratulations, Bucky, m'lad."

Buck lifted his glass. "Let's drink this to Brood Shotwell," he drawled quietly. "A square shooter up against a tough chore, yet playing the game all the way."

Bill Morgan nodded. "Here's to Brood Shotwell."

CHAPTER NINE

Judge Arthur Henning had not been sleeping any too well of late. In fact, it had been months since he had gotten a full, sound night of rest. This uneasiness had come upon him when the trial of Buck Comstock was first in the offing. It had increased as the trial moved on toward its climax. He had had a rotten night after sentence had been passed and when the news came to him that same evening that Buck Comstock had escaped. He had not slept ten minutes all that fateful night. Imagination was playing tricks with the Judge. He had visions of Buck Comstock coming in through a window some night, so the Judge took to locking both door and window and doing a lot of solitary drinking.

As the days went by without Comstock being apprehended or seen, the Judge grew a little more easy in his mind. No doubt Comstock, on escaping from jail, had left the Twin Buttes country for good and all, feeling that a fresh start somewhere else, difficult though it might be to achieve, was infinitely better than twenty-five years in Pinole Penitentiary.

These thoughts were running again through the Judge's mind as he downed another heavy jolt of whiskey and found a slightly unsteady way to bed. The whiskey slugged him to sleep almost immediately.

Sometime later he awoke in stupid, fumbling confusion. There was a loud, peremptory, authoritative knocking at the door. The Judge's heart began to flutter like that of a frightened rabbit. He came perilously close to outright panic. Maybe it was Comstock, coming back in the wee hours of the night to exact vengeance!

The Judge thought of flight, but realized that there was no place to flee to. He thought of opening a window and yelling for help. Yet, disordered and confused as his alcohol drugged brain was, he realized how ridiculous this would make him, if that person knocking at his door was really a legitimate caller.

Shaking and shivering, the Judge crept into his pants and shirt and in a flair of weak defiance, unearthed an old derringer from a bureau drawer. Then he picked up the lamp he had lighted and went to the door.

"Who is it?" he shrilled, trying to keep his voice steady.

"Shotwell," came the answer. "Open up, Judge. I got something important for you to hear."

Tremendous relief flooded the Judge. And because he realized now what a pitiful specimen he had been under the first spasm of his fright, he was harsh and raspy and irascible when he opened his door and was confronted by Sheriff Brood Shotwell and the two cowed and sullen prisoners, Duke Younger and Toad Black.

At sight of the prisoners, the Judge's eyes popped wide, then filmed with a queer and almost frightened wariness. Brood Shotwell, watching Henning closely, did not miss that last expression.

"Sorry to root you out at this time of night, Judge," said Shotwell gruffly. "But these two buzzards got something to say that I want you to hear."

"This is a devilish time to bother me with anything of the sort," snapped the Judge testily. "I'm weary and I need my sleep. You can bring them around again to-morrow, Sheriff."

"I've brought them tonight," Shotwell growled. "This is something that can't wait. It means the righting of a great wrong. So you are going to listen to them. You can," he added sarcastically — "sleep late in the morning."

The Judge tried to meet the boring impact of Shotwell's glance, but failed. His eyes dropped and he stepped aside. "Very well, very well," he exclaimed crustily — "if you insist. But see that all talk is kept down to bare essentials. I'm in no mood for lengthy conversation."

Shotwell herded his prisoners in and closed the door. "All right, Younger," he ordered. "You're first. Speak your little piece. If you think you can clam up and stall, just because Buck Comstock isn't here to work on you — you're all wrong. I'll be glad and eager to take on where Buck left off and to do just about as good a job. Speak up!"

Judge Henning was distinctly startled. "Did you mention Buck Comstock, Sheriff? Where is Comstock? Have you found him?"

"We'll come to that later, Judge," said Shotwell dryly. "Speak up, Younger. Tell the Judge the story, before I get tired of waiting and knock the words loose from you with my fist or a gun barrel."

Younger shifted his feet nervously, stared at the floor. "W-well, Judge — it was like

this. L-Leek Jaeger and Frank Cutts —
they paid me and Black and the other ten
of the jury a hundred simoleons apiece —
to turn in a guilty verdict against — against
Comstock. But, Judge," and here a frantic
pleading note came into his voice — "Us
boys didn't realize —."

"Shut up!" rasped Shotwell. "Well, Judge
— did you get that? Did you hear him say
that Jaeger and Cutts bought that jury for
twelve hundred dollars? That twelve men
— supposedly good and true, sold their
miserable souls and what little personal
honor they might have possessed at one
time, for a filthy hundred dollars apiece?
That they did that so Buck Comstock
would be convicted — railroaded to Pinole?
Now — what have you got to say?"

The Judge had gone pallid, sweat was
starting on his partially bald forehead and
his eyes were blinking wildly. "W— why —
bless — gracious me," he stammered. "I —
I don't know what to say."

"While you're getting back your breath,"
snapped Shotwell with very definite contempt — "we'll listen to Black. All right,
Black — your turn. Is Younger telling the
truth?"

Toad Black, smart enough to know that
he was definitely hooked, and viciously in-

tent on dragging down into the mess everyone else he possibly could, leered savagely as he nodded.

"Sure he's telling the truth. But that ain't news to that bleary-eyed old crane of a Judge. He knew that trial was fixed, all the time he knew it. He knew the jury was bought. And I've been wondering right along how much Jaeger and Cutts paid him to slap twenty-five years on to Comstock. He's the biggest rat of the whole crowd. Me — I took the money they offered me, but they needn't have. I've always hated Buck Comstock's guts — and I always will. I'd have voted him guilty anyhow — money or no money. But a hundred pesos was a hundred pesos and I could make as good use of it as the next hombre. So I took it, just like the rest did. Don't let that old skunk fool you, Shotwell. He's in this every bit as deep as the rest of us — right up to his scrawny old neck. Look at him and you can see that I'm right, the sneaking old hypocrite."

Shotwell did not need a second glance. Judge Arthur Henning seemed to have withered in the space of a few short minutes. The flesh sagged in folds on his cheeks and under his eyes. His lips were shaking and his eyes hunted and frantic.

"That — that's all a lie, a black lie," he gasped. "That leering scoundrel! How dare he make such accusations against me! I'll have him up for contempt. I — I'll sentence him to Pinole for the rest of his natural life —."

"Save your breath, Judge," advised Brood Shotwell curtly. "It looks to me like you are all through sentencing anyone to anywhere. Don't try and lie any more. The truth is in your face."

Judge Arthur Henning sank into a chair, his head in his hands. Confession of his perfidy and knowledge of its enormous effect was written all over him. Sheriff Brood Shotwell's eyes were very, very bleak — and shadowed by a great weariness. He turned to Younger and Black. "You two," he growled — "are traveling. I'm not going to arrest you, though I could, for perjury. But neither of you rats are worth what that trial would cost the county. I don't care where you go, as long as it is plenty far away. You've served your purpose and now I'm giving you a floater. Here I quit talking as a sheriff and for a minute stand as just plain Brood Shotwell, ordinary citizen. And as that citizen I'm telling you something — something you better listen close to — and believe. If, after you walk out of that door, I ever see either of you again within a hundred mile radius of Twin Buttes I'll go for you just like an ordinary citizen. I'll forget all about my star. I won't try and arrest you. I'll just drag a gun and blow you down like I would a sidewinder coiled in a trail." He slid a hand to his gun suggestively. "Git!" he barked flatly.

Younger and Black, startled at their release, but knowing full well that Shotwell meant exactly what he said, shuffled to the door and disappeared in the night. Shotwell shut the door and turned back to Judge Henning. "Well, Judge," he said coldly — "I guess it is your turn to talk — and I reckon you better talk — plenty."

The Judge did not look up, but sat there, head in his hands, hunched shoulders shaking with a kind of queer palsy. "They had me under their thumb," he quavered. "I had to do it, or they would have made a pauper of me. Every cent I have in the world is tied up in . . ."

"Tied up in what?" snapped Shotwell.

The Judge shook his head. He seemed almost on the verge of a stroke. He was shuddering and giving vent to gasping, whimpering moans. The man was far, far gone in the depths of utter cowardice and despair. He was growing incoherent, almost hysterical. Brood Shotwell's eyes glittered with a combination of pity and contempt. It wasn't a pretty sight, to see a man in this shape.

"Before morning, you'll prepare a written authority declaring that past farce no trial," he growled. "You'll dismiss all charges against Buck Comstock and you'll give the reasons why. I'll be in to see you tomorrow some time and I want those papers ready and in order. I'll admit there seems to be a lot of shorthorns in this neck of the woods, but there are a lot of mighty good and square men here also. If I should let out the truth about that trial, it might go plenty hard with you. I'm giving you a chance to clear your dirty skirts a little. Maybe I'm giving you more chance than you deserve."

"My future — my reputation —," whimpered the Judge. "What shall I do — what shall I do — ?"

"That," said Shotwell coldly — "is something you'll have to iron out for yourself, Henning. I hope you notice I'm not calling you Judge, any more. You're not worthy of the name."

At this moment a dark, low crouched figure stole away from the side of the Judge's house, circled a cautious way down to the center of town and finally slipped into the Yellow Horse Saloon. And when, a minute later, Brood Shotwell stepped out into the night, all was empty and still, except for his horse, which stood, patiently ground-reined, rolling its bit ring now and then. The sheriff took up the reins and walked down town, leading the horse behind him, heading for the livery barn at the far end of the street.

A great weariness, a vast disillusionment, lay heavily on Brood Shotwell's drooping shoulders. In his own methodical, undemonstrative way, Brood Shotwell had always worshiped fiercely at the altar of justice as it was first meant to be. For him the dignity and uprightness of the law had been a real and living and spotless thing. For a large part of his life he had served that law and had tried to serve it faithfully.

In all those years he had been in office, he had many, many times seen the mean, leering, naked souls of wayward men paraded before him. He had thought that he had seen the very worst angles of human nature possible. Yet never before had he come across such a foul, crooked mess as now spread its slimy, creeping tentacles all about him. Brood Shotwell was as hardboiled as they came, yet at this moment he felt almost physically sick.

He put up his horse and went to his room. It was very late and he had put in quite a few hard and toilsome days and nights in the past few weeks. Yet he began pacing his room, back and forth, trying to shake himself free of the lethargy of disgust and disillusionment which gripped him.

In the end, the utter, stark physical weariness of the man asserted itself. He threw himself on his bunk and went to sleep. A few hours later, not long before dawn, a faint, muffled thud echoed dimly through the chill darkness. The sound did not awaken Shotwell, though it disturbed him enough to cause him to turn over and sigh deeply, before sinking back once more into heavy sleep. A dog barked fitfully, but even that did not arouse the weary sheriff.

Sheriff Brood Shotwell was up and about again, just after sunup. He was grim of face and eye and his nod was curt to the greetings of several town people he met on the street as he headed for the hashhouse and breakfast. He found his deputy, Spike St. Ives, just finishing eating. Terse and harsh looking as always, St. Ives nodded.

"Morning, Brood. What's the job today?"

"The girl, of course," answered Shotwell. "We got to find that girl."

"Comstock," said St. Ives meaningly — "will be getting plumb away if we don't do something about him."

"Comstock is clear," said Shotwell. "Henning has drawn up papers declaring everything off — a mistrial. He's dismissing all charges against Buck Comstock."

It struck Shotwell that the surprise shown by St. Ives was just a trifle overdone. He shook his head a little savagely. He must be getting morbid. This mess had preyed on his mind until it had him suspecting his own deputy of deceit.

"I ain't the smartest man in the world," said St. Ives. "But I reckon I got a little savvy. Yet, I don't quite savvy this. What happened to make Comstock a free man so sudden?"

"It's like this, Spike," said Shotwell, his tone growing a trifle more mild. "Toad Black and Duke Younger admitted before witnesses that Jaeger and Cutts bought up that jury — paid each of the twelve men a hundred dollars to vote Comstock guilty regardless of what the evidence was." And then he went on to tell the highlights of his experiences the night before, omitting only the truth of Judge

Henning's degradation and deceit.

St. Ives had little to say. The information seemed to floor him. They went out to the street, paused to roll and light smokes. The Widow Jenkins, who eked out a meager living for herself and her three children by doing odd jobs of housework about the town, went hurrying by on her way to Judge Henning's house, where, three times a week she cleaned and scrubbed.

Brood Shotwell thought of Judge Henning as he had last seen him, the night before. A hunched, palsied wretch, stammering out the admission that he had defamed and besmirched his high office. An ugly picture it was, and Shotwell wished he could forget it. He inhaled deeply of his cigarette.

"Yeah," mused the Sheriff. "We go out to find Jean Harper today, Spike. We got to find her. And I'm trying a new hunch today. Buck Comstock gave it to me, last night. I don't mind saying that there is a man with a real head on him. Well, we might as well get the broncs and start —"

He broke off sharply, for, echoing down the street came the shrill, high scream of a terrified woman. Again and again it came and, when they whirled toward the sound, Brood Shotwell and Spike St. Ives saw the

Widow Jenkins come rushing out into the middle of the street, up there at the far end, tossing her arms and shambling about in hysterics.

Shotwell and his deputy raced for the spot and the street behind them filled with a shouting and excited crowd. By the time the sheriff reached the Widow Jenkins, she was on her knees in the dusty street, her apron thrown over her head while she rocked back and forth, moaning. Shotwell caught her by the arms, dragged her to her feet and shook her.

"What's the matter, ma'am," he demanded. "What scared you?"

The widow's eyes rolled, her chin sagged and wobbled. "The Judge," she quavered. "Judge Henning — blood — !"

Shotwell whirled on St. Ives. "Take care of her." Then he darted across to the Judge's house and leaped through the open door. He stopped, dead still.

In one corner of the room was a small desk and chair. In a crumpled heap beside the chair lay Judge Arthur Henning. A dark pool of blood had formed under that prone head. It took Brood Shotwell but a moment to find out two things. Judge Henning was stone dead — and evidently had been, for hours. He had been shot through the head.

Scattered papers, all of them blank, lay on the floor. A bottle of ink had overturned on the desk and spread its crooked, black stain. Some of the ink had run down the slant of the desk and dripped on to the floor.

Sheriff Brood Shotwell turned slowly to the door, where curious and excited men were trying to crowd through. "Get out, boys," rasped the sheriff harshly. "This is a job for the coroner. Somebody has shot Judge Henning. Send the word for Doc Pollard."

As Shotwell got the crowd outside and was about to close the door, Spike St. Ives slipped in. Shotwell locked the door and the two officials went over the room carefully. There was a partially opened window not far from the desk. "Looks like somebody might have inched up outside and shot him through that window," observed St. Ives. "They shore made a dead center bull's-eye," he added callously.

Shotwell, his eyes deep and gleaming, nodded slowly. "They might have been trying to keep him from writing something down," he murmured, as though to himself. "Maybe to keep him from drawing up the clearance papers for Buck Comstock. Black — or Younger — I wonder —."

Doc Pollard pounded at the door and was admitted. His examination was swift. As he finished and stood up, Shotwell spoke. "About when would you say it happened, Doc?"

"Off-hand, around one or two o'clock this morning. And say, Brood — you know what my wife was telling me at breakfast this morning — hell, it wasn't five minutes before this call came for me. Well — she told me that about half past one this morning something woke her up and she was kind of half conscious of it being a shot. Maybe she heard the very shot that killed the Judge."

"Maybe she did," nodded the sheriff. "Well, Doc, you take charge and make arrangements for the inquest. In the meantime I'll be looking into things and runing down a couple of ideas."

"Wonder who could have done it?" said Doc.

Shotwell shrugged wearily. "God knows. This damned country has gone crazy and it's driving me the same way."

Some time later Shotwell and St. Ives mounted horses in front of the livery barn and rode out of Twin Buttes. They rode alone, taking no posse with them. Two miles out they met up with Leek Jaeger,

Frank Cutts and Whistler Hahn, who were heading for town at a leisurely pace. Shotwell spoke a quick aside to his deputy. "Let me do all the talking, Spike."

Jaeger, Cutts and Hahn reined in. "Where away this morning, Shotwell?" demanded Jaeger. "Going to make another try for Comstock?"

Shotwell shook his head. "Got more recent things to worry about," he growled. "I'm hunting two things — that girl — and the jasper who shot Judge Henning last night."

The three men jerked upright in their saddles. "What's that?" barked Jaeger. "You trying to tell us that Judge Henning was shot — killed?"

"That's what. Somebody shot him last night, late — while he was sitting at his desk at home. Widow Jenkins, who did the housework for him, found the body this morning. Doc Pollard said the Judge had been dead for hours."

"But who in hell would have wanted to plug Judge Henning?" blurted Jaeger.

"I'm trying to figure that out myself," said Shotwell quietly. "At present, all I know is — somebody did."

"More than one criminal who the Judge has sent over the road, could have had it in for him," Cutts observed coldly.

Leek Jaeger jerked around in his saddle. "By God!" he exclaimed. "I bet you've hit the answer, Frank."

"Meaning what?" rasped Shotwell.

"Comstock, you fool. Buck Comstock. He'd be feeling that way toward Judge Henning. I tell you, Shotwell — you better —."

Shotwell cut him short with a curt laugh. "Suppose we lay off that kind of talk, Jaeger — until we're damned certain. It strikes me you're a little too ready in your accusations against Buck Comstock. You've made talk that Comstock was the one who ran off with Jean Harper. Now you got him murdering Judge Henning. And you backed the charge of him murdering Ben Sloan. I'd go a little slow, was I you — else some of these wild accusations are liable to develop a kickback."

Quick anger twisted the blocky features of Leek Jaeger. "Do I have to remind you again, Shotwell — that election is only three months off? Don't you try and threaten me."

"Listen, Jaeger," said Shotwell, and there was something in his voice which Jaeger had never heard there before. "You've made that same kind of a crack to me before. Now I'll tell you something and I want you to listen careful and get all of it. Whether I'm sheriff after next election isn't worrying me a damn, right now. Until the voters on this range decide they want a different man in office, I'll keep on packing this star. And Jaeger — while I'm sheriff — I aim to be sheriff — all the way. Get that — all the way.

"Me, I haven't been making much talk, but I've been riding and I've been looking and I've been listening. And I've discovered that there are more low-down skunks in this neck of the woods than you could shake a stick at. Jaeger, you tend to your business and I'll tend to mine."

Jaeger would have made another retort, but Frank Cutts threw up his hand. "Shut up, Leek. You had that call down coming. Brood is doing all right. I'd like to ask one question, though. You got any line at all on Comstock, Shotwell?"

"I might have," answered Shotwell, looking Cutts hard in the eye. "Yeah, I might have. You'll hear about it, later on. Come on, Spike — we got work to do."

Leek Jaeger watched the sheriff and his deputy ride off, his little, lead colored eyes hard and calculating. "That hombre shows signs of getting ructious," he growled. "We may have to put some real pressure on him before long."

"I don't blame him a bit for getting his roach up," said Cutts angrily. "Damn it all, Leek — won't you ever learn to keep your mouth shut? You got the meanest mouth I ever saw on a man. You'd antagonize a saint. When are you ever going to learn that you can catch a lot more flies with honey than you can with vinegar?"

"Right," broke in Whistler Hahn, in his queer, sibilant, hissing tone. "I been around, more or less, and I can tell you this much. More men have talked their way into a grave than ever argued their way out. Unless you got plenty of guns to back it up, a close mouth is the best life insurance I know."

Jaeger's neck was swollen and red with anger, but he bit back the words he wanted to speak and spurred his horse ahead toward town. Cutts and Hahn followed, at a more leisurely pace.

Brood Shotwell, his face harsh and bitter, rode south for the entire length of Timber Valley, with Spike St. Ives jogging silently along at his elbow. They had spoken not at all since the meeting with Jaeger and Cutts and Whistler Hahn. Shotwell was grimly thoughtful. St. Ives rode with his lank figure in a crouching slouch, his narrow face inscrutable and expressionless. At length, as the miles kept reeling back, St. Ives stirred restlessly.

"Just where in hell are we heading, anyhow?" he asked.

"I want to check up on something — concerning the disappearance of Jean Harper," answered Shotwell. "You ought to be able to see by this time, Spike — that something is mighty rotten around this range, some central purpose that has been stirring up all this trouble. No, I don't believe it is Comstock — in fact I know it's not. As I see it, the answer to the whole mess will come right out in the open when we locate that girl and have a chance to talk to her. So, I'm running down a little hunch this morning."

St. Ives built a cigarette. "What makes you think you might find the girl down in this direction?"

Shotwell shrugged. "I said I had a hunch, didn't I," he answered irritably. "That girl is being hid out, somewhere on this range. No other answer makes sense. We've just about checked up on everything else — but the different ranchhouses. We're going to search every ranch on the range, starting with the Stirrup Cross."

St. Ives gave an imperceptible start and looked guardedly at Shotwell from the corner of his eye. "Hell! You don't think that old Tom Addis knows anything about the disappearance of that girl, do you?"

Shotwell shrugged again. "All I'm thinking is that I ain't been thinking deep enough or along the right line, so far. But I'm starting to — now."

Shotwell pulled gradually to the east, leaving Timber Valley and crossing the barren stagehand beyond, to come down into the southern portion of Coyote Valley. Out there, dead ahead, stood the headquarters of the Stirrup Cross.

Spike St. Ives tugged his battered hat low over his eyes, as though to hide the spark of red fire which had begun to burn, far back in them. He shifted slightly sideways in the saddle.

As they jogged up in front of the Stirrup Cross ranchhouse, old man Addis came out to meet them. Addis looked worried and seedy. His manner and voice were querulous and uneasy.

"Morning, Shotwell," he grumbled. "What brings you down this way?"

The vast uneasiness of the man was plainly discernible in the irascible tone and the shifting flicker of the washed out eyes.

Brood Shotwell's own eyes narrowed as he dismounted.

"I'm looking for Jean Harper, Addis," he said gruffly. "I got to thinking that she might be hid out in one of the ranchhouses somewhere along this range. So I'm going to search 'em — all. I'm starting in on your spread."

Addis went white as a sheet. He began to shake. "I didn't want them to bring her here," he quavered. "I told them not to — but damn 'em, they did anyhow. I'm not a party to this thing, Shotwell. I swear I'm not. I couldn't help myself. They made me do it. They had me pinched where I couldn't get away. And I knew this would happen — I knew this would happen."

He began wringing his hands in a manner which reminded Shotwell of how Judge Henning had caved. Shotwell knew a sudden, lashing ferocity. He would liked to have taken Addis by the throat and twisted his skinny neck for him. How far, in God's name, did this cesspool of deceit and corruption reach? Who next would he find to be still another tool of greed and fear?

Without looking back, he spoke harshly over his shoulder to St. Ives. "Come on, Spike. We've found the answer to one of our problems. Get out of your saddle and help me search this ranchhouse."

Instead of obeying, Spike St. Ives slipped a gun free. His voice was thin and venomous. "You're hitting too close to the truth, Shotwell. Sorry."

And then he shot Sheriff Brood Shotwell through the body!

The sheriff lurched, coughed, weaved and went down.

Even as Shotwell struck the ground, from the head of the low slope above the ranchhouse, a rifle snarled wickedly. Speeding lead told with a vicious slap. The impact seemed to lift Spike St. Ives completely out of his saddle and he went down in a whirl of limp arms and legs. St. Ives was stone dead when he crashed to earth.

Brood Shotwell, lanced through and through by the bitter agony of that treacherous lead that St. Ives had thrown, his senses blurred and fading, managed by terrific effort to pull himself up on one elbow. Through the darkness which was closing in across his eyes he could dimly see a compact body of riders, lashing down the slope, and he could hear the mutter of speeding hoofs. He did not understand — he could not understand.

Then his elbow caved under him and the last thing he knew was the terrified bleat of old man Addis, ringing faintly in his ears.

CHAPTER TEN

For a long time after Sheriff Brood Shotwell had ridden away toward town with his two prisoners, Duke Younger and Toad Black — Buck Comstock, Bill Morgan and Bones Baker sat talking in the Circle Star ranch-house. When they drank their first glass as a toast to the sheriff, Bones hurried to refill the glasses.

"Drink hearty, men," chirruped Bones. "When this bottle is empty, I'll rustle another. Me — I feel like going on a binge to celebrate. By gollies — I shore do. Buck, maybe you better let me take a look at that leg of yours where Black kicked you. Doggone his crooked soul — I wish I'd batted him a little harder with my frying pan the other day."

Buck laughed softly and vetoed both suggestions. "The leg is all right, Bones — and don't worry about another bottle. We aren't going to more than dent this one. Got more important things to think of than whiskey. Bill, do you realize that I'm a free man once more?"

"That's right," agreed Morgan. "I shore do. Just the same, don't get reckless about it, Buck. Not having Brood after you any more doesn't mean you're plumb clear of trouble, Buck. Jaeger and Cutts, when they hear about it, will be after your scalp — plenty. Always remember, that as long as those two whelps are running free and wild, you want to keep off the top of ridges. Yes sir, they'll shore be after your scalp with a vengeance, now."

"And I'll be after their scalps," drawled Buck with ominous quiet. "The picture keeps on clearing up, Bill. We got those two buzzards in the open now — and we know for certain what they're after. There ain't the slightest doubt in my mind but that they're behind the disappearance of Jean Harper."

"They seem to be in back of every other piece of dirty work," nodded Morgan. "I'd give a lot to know what became of that girl."

Buck's jaw stole out. "The very first thing I intend to do is run that trail down. For all we know, she may be hid out somewhere in the J Bar C ranchhouse, or at some other ranch on this range. She's around here, somewhere. I — I kind of feel it, somehow."

"Common sense narrows the whole thing down pretty well," observed Bill Morgan dryly. "We know she's not in this house. And we know she wouldn't be at the Rafter T or the Lazy F. Bud Tharp and Johnny Frazier just don't shape up that way, Buck."

"Hell!" growled Buck. "I know that. But I'm going to have a good look at the Wineglass again. And they might even have brass enough to have her hid out in my own cabin, sort of hoping maybe that she'd be found there and that I'd get the blame. You can't tell what deviltry Jaeger and Cutts would think up after all we know now. Anyway, I shore am going to have a good look around."

"How come in all this talk you don't mention the Stirrup Cross," put in Bones Baker. "There's a ranchhouse down there, you know. Or don't you figure old man Addis would be mixed up —."

Buck snorted contemptuously. "Old man Addis is a whining, cantankerous old pelican, but he ain't got the nerve of a field mouse, I don't think —."

Bill Morgan jumped to his feet, took a quick turn up and down the room. "Wait a minute — wait a minute," he rumbled. "That reminds me — that makes me think. Buck — you remember the night I met you out at Indian Spring? I told you then how I'd sort of mixed my trail up after leaving here. How I wandered clear down to the Stirrup Cross and how I run across Jaeger and Cutts there, talking to Tom Addis. None of the three seemed any way over-joyed at seeing me, and Jaeger and I had a little word fuss over you. And the funny part of it was, after Jaeger and Cutts rode off and I stayed and tried to talk easy and friendly with Addis, he was miffed as hell because I'd called Jaeger down. In other words, Addis sided in with those other two pole cats. At the time it struck me as powerful queer, but afterwards, I forgot it. When Bones just mentioned the Stirrup Cross, I remembered again. If," he added meaningly, stopping his pacing to stare at Buck shrewdly — "if you're going to search ranchhouse, I wouldn't overlook the Stirrup Cross."

Buck's eyes gleamed. "Keno! First thing tomorrow morning we'll have a little look through the Stirrup Cross. And if we find Jean Harper there, Tom Addis is going to have his scrawny neck stretched. If Miss Harper ain't there — the next place we tackle is the J Bar C."

Morgan nodded slowly. "That last listens like quite a chore to me, Buck. It will take more than a couple of us to put that over."

"I reckon maybe Bud Tharp and Johnny Frazier will be interested too."

"Correct. But even that won't be a big enough showing to guarantee a safe skin around the J Bar C. I reckon it would be wise to take along some of the crew, too. A dozen of us won't make too many if and when we hit the J Bar C."

"Take along all you think are necessary, Bill," Buck said, yawning. "Well, I'm going to turn in. Tonight I sleep on a real bunk again. It's been quite a hell of a long time since I knew that luxury — and I feel like I could stand it."

The following morning, with two of the Circle Star riders, Buck Comstock and Bill Morgan rode south to the Rafter T, where they put their plan before Bud Tharp. Bud, short and broad, was explosively happy over Buck's exoneration by Brood Shotwell.

"Brood is square," averred Bud Tharp. "I admit I had my doubts a couple of times, but I'm frank to admit I was wrong. Most likely, what with all he found out listening to Black and Younger talk, Brood is beginning to get an idea on a lot of crooked stuff that has happened on this range ever since Jaeger and Cutts first got together in their rotten combine. Shore, I'll go along with you boys and I'll throw a couple of my punchers into the gang."

From the Rafter T they went to the Lazy F and were met by the same kind of welcome. Johnny Frazier, tall and keen eyed, spoke with a soft, lazy drawl as he showed real enthusiasm for the scheme. "Even," he said, "if we don't draw a lick of luck, there'll be a lot of satisfaction in showing Jaeger and Cutts that we got our suspicions and that we ain't afraid to back them up. Me — I'm going to enjoy this."

When they left the Lazy F, they mustered ten men. Buck, leading the pack, knew a swelling, pulse tingling exultation. How good it was to ride like this, backed by nine tried and true men who would fight with him and for him to the last fringe of hell! The solitary trail of the fugitive, of the hunted, was no longer his bitter portion. He set a burning pace for the Stirrup Cross. It had taken quite a bit of time, telling Bud and Johnny all about things and getting the punchers armed and mustered to ride. The sun was already pretty high in its climb. And there was so much to do.

Just short of the crest of the low slope above the Stirrup Cross ranchhouse, the crest which hid their approach, Buck halted the others, then went on alone to look things over. There was no sense in charging blindly down on the place. So many queer, underhand things were going on, a man never knew what he might run into. And while Buck was impatient to see a great many things done, he was not going to let that impatience lead him into fool-hardiness. So, some twenty yards back from the crest he left his horse and went forward on foot, crouched and wary.

As he peered over the crest and down the slope, he saw something which startled him. Two riders were moving in on the ranchhouse from the north west. Buck identified Brood Shotwell and his deputy, Spike St. Ives. Neither sheriff nor deputy looked right or left, but headed straight on for the ranchhouse. Buck turned and waved his party up, stepping back to get his horse and swing into the saddle.

"Shotwell and St. Ives just rode in down there," he said. "I guess Brood is out to do a little searching on his own, Bill. Remember, I suggested it to him, last night."

"Correct," nodded Bill Morgan. "Looks like we had our ride down here for nothing. Brood can take care of this outfit, all right."

"We'll stick around a minute or two," said Buck. "I'm curious to find out if Brood runs across anything."

The group of riders moved up to the crest and watched Shotwell and St. Ives pull to a halt by the ranchhouse. They saw old Tom Addis advance at his stiff, shuffling walk to speak to the two. They saw Brood Shotwell dismount, talk for a moment to Addis, who began to cringe and wring his hands. And then, as Brood Shotwell swung past Addis, as though to go into the ranchhouse, Buck and his crowd saw Spike St. Ives whip out a gun and shoot Brood Shotwell down.

But Tharp, who had been carrying his Winchester across the saddle in front of him, reacted with automatic and bewildering speed. Even before the first cough of report had died from the treacherous deputy's gun, Bud tossed up his rifle and it spat a thin, ringing challenge. Spike St. Ives went from his saddle like something poleaxed with lightning.

"The damned, rotten dog," cried Bud Tharp. "He shot Brood in the back."

The next moment the entire group of riders was spurring down the slope. Buck,

228

his heart cold with dread and fury, rode in the van, his eyes fixed on Brood Shotwell. He saw the sheriff pull himself up on one elbow, then collapse again. A moment later Buck was out of his saddle and on his knees beside Shotwell.

The sheriff was unconscious, but not dead. Yet he was wickedly wounded. The treacherous slug from the gun of Spike St. Ives had struck him just below and to the back of the right shoulder and had ranged downward. Johnny Frazier, helping Buck, swore softly and shook his head as he saw the wound. "Looks bad," he growled. "Damned bad. Brood ain't as young as he used to be."

"We got to do all we can," gritted Buck. "Oh — that damned, treacherous rat of a St. Ives — to shoot a man like Brood Shotwell — shoot him in the back. And Brood had worked with him, paid him wages — trusted him. Gawd! How low some men can sink! Did Bud make a center shot on St. Ives?"

"Plenty, I'd say," nodded Frazier. "Like to tore him in half. Bud saved us the chore of swinging him."

Bill Morgan came rushing up, pushed Buck aside, dropping down beside the wounded sheriff. "I'll help Johnny take care of Brood," he rumbled. "You go talk to Addis, Buck. I think he's got something interesting to tell you."

Buck, a little bewildered, found Bud Tharp holding a gun on Addis, who seemed to be having a fit of the ague. The ranch owner was shivering and shaking, twisting his hands and making strange whimpering noises to himself. Farther over, three riders who worked for Addis, puzzled and angry and wondering, were being held under the guns of the rest of Buck's party.

"What's Addis got to say, Bud?" demanded Buck.

"Looks like we came to the right place," growled Bud Tharp. "Addis has got that Harper girl locked up in the house, Buck. He's trying to swear something or other, but he's got the shakes so bad you can't make much sense out of him."

Buck caught Addis by the shoulder and shook the man savagely. "Get hold of yourself, Addis," he rasped. "You're in a damned tight spot. You better talk and talk plenty. What's this about Miss Harper being at this ranch?"

Add is jerked a thumb toward the house. "She — she's in there," he stammered. "Jaeger — Cutts — brought her in here.

They — they put her in my — my store-room. They m-made me do it. They made me — d-damn their black souls! They been ironing me down and down — and now —"

Addis began to shake again and his ordinarily tight chin became so loose and wobbly his words ran off into an unintelligible mutter. In seething disgust, Buck threw him aside. "Keep a gun on him, Bud. When he quits shaking, we're going to learn a lot from that jasper."

Buck ran to the house then and leaped in. More than once he had been in the Stirrup Cross ranchhouse, back in the old days before the curse of Jaeger and Cutts came to throw the shadow of deceit and crookedness over everything they looked at. He knew where the storeroom was. He stopped before the door of it, noted the heavy hasp and padlock. A cold, white rage swayed Buck. Somehow, the thought of that slim, black-haired girl, held like some criminal or wild animal behind that padlock, reached far down into Buck and stirred to life a fury and resentment the like of which he had never experienced before. And it was Jaeger and Cutts who had done this. He'd remember it, when he finally met up with them for a showdown.

He knocked on the door and called out, "Miss Harper — Miss Harper! This is Buck Comstock!"

He heard her muffled cry of surprise and relief. He heard her beat her little fists on the inner side of that padlocked door.

"B-Buck — Buck Comstock!" came her muffled voice. "Oh — Buck, get me out of here — get me out of here!"

Buck tore for the kitchen and found a heavy, iron poker. Back at the storeroom door he went to work. He jammed the end of the poker under the hasp and began to pry. The set of that hasp was stout and stubborn, but Buck was full of the furious strength of anger. He wedged the poker to a better purchase and set back with all his power and weight. Sounded the slow, squealing pull of straining staple and bolt — the splintering of wood. Then the hasp clanged loose and free. Buck pushed the door open.

She stood there for a moment, tousled and disheveled, looking at him with eyes that were wide and swimming with emotion. She was twisting her slim hands. Her soft, puckered lower lip began to tremble like that of a hurt child. "B-Buck," she whispered. "Oh — Buck, I knew you'd come for me."

Then she ran to him and crept into his arms. She clung to him and began to sob convulsively. Buck stood very tall and straight and still, holding her like he might some terrified child, saying no word but patting her on the shoulder in an awkward attempt to comfort her.

A mixture of thoughts jumbled Buck's mind. How little and slim she was — Jaeger and Cutts, he'd have their damned hearts for this — there was a subtle, haunting fragrance to that dark, tousled head burrowed against his shoulder — he'd see that Tom Addis was hung for his part — he wished she wouldn't sob like that and that he wasn't so damned tongue-tied so he could say something which might help.

As abruptly as she had given way, she quieted. She pulled apart from him, daubing at her eyes. "I — I'm sorry," she whispered. "I — I didn't mean to go to pieces, like that. But the relief — to know that a friend — to know that I'd be out of there — out of that room —." She choked up again.

Buck found his tongue at last. "I savvy," he drawled gently. "All things considered, you're a mighty brave little lady. Later, when you're feeling better, you can tell me how it all happened."

"I'll tell you now." She spoke swiftly, intensely, as though it was a vast relief. And she told him how Cutts and Jaeger had overpowered her, tricked her, at the J Bar C ranchhouse — and told of the long ride through the night, bound hand and foot and head muffled in a Navajo blanket so that she could not see where they were bound. "I had not the slightest idea where I was," she went on. "I saw nothing until they took the blanket off my head when they had me in that room. And the window of that room, it was boarded up. I could see a little sunshine come through the cracks and I could see one end of a corral and part of a feed shed. But that told me nothing."

"Of course," prompted Buck tersely, "the whole idea of Cutts and Jaeger was to try and force you to sell your ranch to them at their price? Right?"

"Yes. Right. They threatened me and bulldozed me, trying to get me to sell at their figure. I — I told them that I wouldn't sell to them if they offered me a million dollars."

"Good girl. Did Addis bother you in any way? We've got him outside right now and the boys are thinking strong of a lynch rope and a tree."

"No — no!" she cried. "You mustn't harm Mr. Addis. He was good to me — kind to me. He brought me my meals. He always seemed so frightened and nervous about the whole thing. But it was Mr. Addis who came in that morning with a gun when Cutts — when Cutts —." Her voice frittered thinly out and the pallor of her face deepened.

"Yes," prompted Buck, his voice gentle, but his eyes going bleak as ice. "What about — Cutts?"

"He came in one morning — and threatened me — again," she went on, her voice little more than a whisper. "I — I defied him and I told him that for carrying me off this way — he'd be hung. He seemed to go crazy when I told him that. He became an evil, savage beast. I fought him and fought him. I — I bit his hand when he tried to keep me from crying for help. Then he hit me, with his fist. Addis — Mr. Addis came in then, with a gun. And he told Cutts he'd kill him, if he ever tried to lay a finger on me again. So — you see — you mustn't harm — Mr. Addis."

"I see," said Buck hoarsely. He was dizzy with the fury that rippled through him like scalding metal. "Cutts — will hang — he'll hang. I'll see that your promise is made good. God yes — how high he'll hang — and how long. You — you stay here and pull yourself together. I got business outside with the boys. I'll be back for you in a minute and we'll take you to Bill Morgan's ranch, where nothing can ever frighten or harm you again."

He stumbled a little as he went out, half blind with the torrent of feeling which racked him. Cutts — he'd struck Jean — struck her with his fist. And only Tom Addis — with a gun —.

The bright flare of the sun outside seemed to clear Buck's head and eyes somewhat. He saw that a blanket litter was being swung between two horses, evidently to carry Brood Shotwell. Bud Tharp still held a gun on old man Addis.

"The girl all right, Buck?" asked Bud. "On your answer depends whether this damned old coyote goes on living."

"You can put up your gun, Bud," answered Buck harshly. "Miss Harper is all right. She'll be out in a minute." Buck bent cold eyes on Tom Addis. "How long you been in cahoots with Jaeger and Cutts?"

"I'm not in cahoots with them," Addis cried. "They made me keep that poor girl prisoner. They made me, I tell you." Addis had steadied a lot by this time.

"That," growled Buck — "sounds like poor talk to me, Addis. How could they *make* you do a thing of this sort?"

"How? Look! This ranch," and Addis waved an encircling hand — "This ranch is all I have. The best part of my life went into building this ranch. Jaeger and Cutts threatened to drive me to the wall — to take it away from me. And they could do it, too. They have the men, the money, the power. What could I do? My partner and myself —."

"Your what?" cut in Buck. "Since when did you have a partner?"

"I've had one for years. No one knew of it besides Judge Henning and myself. How Jaeger and Cutts found it out I don't know — and I still don't know. But some way they did."

"Where does Judge Henning come into the picture? Why should he know something that was secret to so many others?"

"Judge Henning is my partner," declared Addis. "All he and I own in this world is tied up in this ranch. We're old men — too old to fight a combine like Jaeger and Cutts. What could we do under the threat of their power?"

"Judge Henning!" breathed Buck. "Judge Henning — your partner! Ah —

that does make the picture complete. I see it now — I see the whole thing."

One of Bill Morgan's riders came over to them. "Those three Stirrup Cross punchers want to talk to you, Buck."

Buck nodded and followed the rider over to where the three men stood. Buck knew these boys. Andy Perrine, Sig Loftus and Dave Burke. Andy Perrine spoke.

"Buck, I want you to believe me when I say that neither Sig or Dave or I had any idea at all that that girl was locked up in the old man's storeroom. None of us go into the main house, not once in a month of Sundays. If we'd known she was there we shore as hell would have tore the roof off. We knew something was on the mind of Addis, for he acted worried and scared and crotchety. But we figured he'd probably gotten into some kind of a business deal with Cutts and Jaeger and was getting his hide skinned off, them two being the kind of crooked whelps they are. That, of course, was none of our affair. We're hired to punch cattle, not to iron out the business troubles of the boss. That's how we were looking at things. And we positively didn't know a thing about the girl. That's gospel, Buck."

Buck nodded gravely. "I believe you,

Andy. We're holding nothing against you three. You can go or stay or do as you please."

"Me," growled Dave Burke — "I'm leaving. I wouldn't stay on with any damn man who'd do what Tom Addis has done. I'm drawing my time — plumb immediate. When I ride, I want to ride for a man with sand in his craw — not for some damned spineless old jellyfish. What the hell made him do it, anyhow?"

Buck told them, briefly — what Addis had just told him. "In a way, I can see his point, boys. Tom Addis is an old man. Give him a little the best of the doubt. And I happen to know that he was more than kind to Miss Harper and that he threw a gun on Cutts one day to make him behave."

"That girl," asked Sig Loftus. "Did Jaeger or Cutts really hurt her in any way? If they did, by Gawd — I'm going scalp hunting — starting now!"

"Miss Harper is all right," said Buck. "But I'm saying this. From here on out it is open season on either Jaeger or Cutts. No matter where you run across 'em — if you do, just draw down and kill 'em. Don't stop to ask questions or say a word. Just throw lead and make it good. For there are two coyotes whose hides need hanging up, boys. It is going to have to be done if this range is to be a fit place to live on. Now if you fellows want to help out in that chore, we'll be more than glad to have you tie in with Bill and Bud and Johnny and me."

"We're in — right up to our necks," exclaimed Andy Perrine. "We're with you, Buck — all the way. Where do we start?"

"Right at this ranch. You stay here. Forget about handling cattle for a few days. Keep Winchesters handy and don't let either Jaeger or Cutts or any of their outfit within rifle shot of this place. They're out to hog this whole range, and we can't afford to let them get an extra foothold anywhere. There's a lot going on boys, that you never dreamed about. You'll have to take my word for it. You make damn certain that they don't dig in here and you'll be helping more than you guess."

"I'll see that it's done," growled Dave Burke. "Don't worry none about this spread, Buck. How about the old man?"

"He'll stay here, too. I think this scare has pounded some sense, and maybe a little backbone into him. I think he'll be willing to fight, now."

Buck went over to where Bill Morgan

and Johnny Frazier had just lifted Brood Shotwell into the litter. "How's he making it?" asked Buck.

"Pretty fair, near as I can tell," said Morgan. "We're taking him to my place. I've sent Gus Howard to town for Doc Pollard. They'll probably be waiting at the ranch time we get there. The girl all right?"

"Yeah — she's fine. I didn't want to bring her out here with a wounded man and a dead one lying around. Soon as we get St. Ives out of the way, I'll get her. I'm bringing her out to the Circle Star, too, Bill. She's got plenty of spunk. She'll make a good nurse for Brood."

Morgan and Frazier got under way with the wounded sheriff, horses moving at a slow walk. At Buck's command the three Stirrup Cross boys took charge of the body of Spike St. Ives, as ugly in death as it had been in life.

"What'll we do with him?" asked Sig Loftus. "A crooked, shoot a man in the back sort like St. Ives, hardly deserves burying."

"It's got to be done," said Buck grimly. "A little pick and shovel work for you fellows. Select your own spot."

The body was carried away and Buck

went into the house after Jean Harper. She was waiting for him and by some feminine legerdemain had succeeded in making herself neat and trim looking. There was some color in her cheeks now, but her eyes, as Buck looked at her admiringly, turned shy.

All set," exclaimed Buck heartily. "We're ready to ride."

As they went out, they met old man Addis. There was a new look about the old rancher now. He no longer cringed and his head was carried higher. It was as if, now that everything was known, some tremendous load had been lifted from his shoulders. He looked at Jean and spoke directly to her.

"Miss," he said simply. "I don't deserve any kindness from you — none at all. Yet I'm hoping you'll find it in your heart to forgive an old man who's been a fool and a spineless coward, but who's got a little manhood back. And I want you to know, that even if you were locked up in my house, they'd have had to kill me before they could have done you any real harm."

Even Buck, savage as was the turmoil still raging in him, knew a little pity for Tom Addis at that moment. And Jean — she smiled gravely at the old fellow and held out her hand. "As far as I am concerned, you're my very good friend, Mr. Addis," she told him. "You were in a position where you could hardly help yourself and, after that morning when you drove Cutts off at the point of a gun, I knew that you'd not let anything happen to me. Yes, you and I are friends."

Addis gulped and blinked, then peered a little fearfully at Buck, who put out his hand. "Shake, Tom. The past is dead. The future is a brand new picture. You and I — we'll get along."

"Th— thanks, Buck," stuttered the old man.

They rode away from the Stirrup Cross together, just the two of them, side by side — for Morgan and Tharp and Frazier and the others had already left. Buck, glancing at the girl beside him, could hardly believe she could have been the wan, tremulous, tearful youngster who had faced him when he opened the door of her prison.

Now her head was high again and her cheeks washed with warm color. The shadow which had been in her eyes was gone and an eagerness had taken its place. It was as if she had somehow achieved a great wisdom during her long hours of imprisonment and was now facing the future fortified by the strength of that wisdom.

Her lips parted slightly to the gentle lash of the warm, free air and tendrils of dark hair whipped about her face.

They soon caught up with the others, for Bill Morgan was holding down the pace, to give as much comfort as possible to the wounded sheriff. Jean Harper's face sobered as she glimpsed that limp figure swinging in the blanket between the two horses.

"D— dead?" she asked Buck gravely.

"No. But badly wounded. His own deputy, crooked whelp that he was, shot Brood in the back. We're taking him to the Circle Star. Bill Morgan has already sent a rider to town after Doc Pollard. Do you think you could qualify as a nurse?"

"I'd like to try," she nodded. "You see, I understand in a general way now, the battle which is going on across this range. I am in it now, on your side. I want to help. For it is my battle, as well as yours."

"You're becoming quite a Westerner," Buck drawled, a teasing note in his voice.

She shrugged, her face sober. "I'm not at all the person who stood in the courtroom that day. I'm no longer remotely like that person. I see life as I never saw it before and recognize its responsibilities. There is a fierce strength about your range country,

Buck Comstock, which molds people swiftly to its needs."

"It's a good country, when you learn to know it," said Buck. "You've got the strength and nerve to fit into the picture."

Her color deepened and her eyes took on a brooding content.

CHAPTER ELEVEN

Doc Pollard, stocky, cheerful and ruddy faced, came out of the sick room, wiping his hands on a towel.

"What are his chances, Doc?" asked Buck Comstock.

"Fifty-fifty. Brood is a tough old wolf. I got the slug. The good Lord must have guided that bullet. An inch right or left and Shotwell would have been dead, hours ago. I'll have a better idea about twenty-four hours from now. Right now I'm some worried, but not too much. That girl is a dandy, a spunky little monkey. Having her here to nurse Brood won't hurt his chances any."

Buck went outside and relayed this news to Bill Morgan, Johnny Frazier and Bud Tharp, who had been discussing the mysterious killing of Judge Henning, the news of which had been brought from town by Doc Pollard. They nodded in relief at Buck's message.

"That's mighty fine," said Johnny Frazier. "Brood is too good a man to die. And now that that is settled, where do we go from here?"

Buck put his hand in his pocket, turned to Bill Morgan and with a swift movement pinned something on Morgan's shirt. It was a nickeled, ball-pointed star — a sheriff's star. "I took that off of Brood when I first went looking for his wound," Buck told his startled audience. "Right now, this county needs a sheriff — and law; the kind of law that Jaeger and Cutts can't bluff, buy or dodge. Brood Shotwell is down on his back and due to stay there for quite a spell. St. Ives, the treacherous skunk, is dead. If Brood was able to talk, I know damn well he'd be more than willing to see Bill wear this star and go on with the job of cleaning house.

"We know that all of this crowd can be trusted. In the light of all the things that have happened, that's a plenty important item. Bill here, is the oldest, most level headed of this crowd. Everybody knows him and he packs a lot of weight. Let him wear that star, call us the posse, and we go get Jaeger and Cutts. We got absolute proof that they run off with Jean Harper. That's plenty of cause and charge for their arrest. I say, let's pool all the outfits and go get 'em. Let's carry this fight right into their faces and jam it down their throats. What do you say, boys?"

"Keno!" rasped Bud Tharp harshly. "The only way to beat a pair of schemers like those two is to hit 'em when they ain't expecting it and then keep on hitting 'em until you get 'em down. I'm all in favor of what Buck suggests."

"And me," said Johnny Frazier.

Bill Morgan nodded slowly. "With you boys behind me I'd tackle a nest of poison wild-cats. Bud — Johnny, when you send for your crews, I'd suggest you leave a couple of men at each ranch, just in case. When Jaeger and Cutts find out how bad things are breaking for them, there's no telling what they might try in an effort to whip us. I wouldn't put it past 'em to try and burn out all of us."

Eager riders, ears burning with instructions from their bosses, tore for the Rafter T and Lazy F. At the Circle Star preparations went forward quietly. Fresh horses were roped and held ready for the saddle. Weapons were overhauled and belt loops plugged full of fresh ammunition.

Buck Comstock's pulse had stepped up to an eager tempo. At last he was going to be able to hit straight out at the two rascals who had come so close to robbing him of his liberty — his future — the schemers who had corrupted and ruined men who had been good and true before. The shadow of Jaeger and Cutts had spread across the Twin Buttes range like some malignant plague, soiling and debasing all it touched.

Now the strong, clean wind of law and order and righteousness was about to pour the power of its breath on that plague. Honest guns were massing to back up that power. Up until now the J Bar C crowd had done the attacking, had poured on the pressure. Now it would be the other way around and Buck wondered how Jaeger and Cutts would react when they were driven into a corner and the shadow of the rope was reaching for them. What would become of the strut and swagger and bluster of Leek Jaeger? And would that sleek, cold suavity of Frank Cutts drop from him? Time would tell, and Buck promised himself savagely that he'd be there to see the unveiling of those two renegades.

It was getting on toward midafternoon when the Rafter T and Lazy F riders came thundering in. Bill Morgan made ready to ride immediately. He turned to Gus Howard, his foreman. "Tell Goober and Sleepy to stay here with Bones, Gus. The rest of us ride."

They pounded away from the Circle Star, angling north and west. They poured up out of Coyote Valley and out on to the sage tableland. Far up there, swimming in the heat mists, loomed East Butte and West Butte. And up near those buttes and slightly to the east of them, a long, low cloud of yellow dust peeled like a ribbon across the world.

Of those pounding riders, none seemed to pay any attention to that ribbon of dust except Buck Comstock. But that dust puzzled Buck. There was just one answer to it. Cattle! A big herd of them, traveling east. What cattle — and going — where?

Buck's eyes narrowed, his jaw hardened in sudden understanding. He sank in the spurs, raced up beside Bill Morgan and caught him by the arm. "Pull up, Bill — pull up!" he yelled.

The thundering cavalcade slowed to a jog. Buck pointed. "That dust, Bill. It means cattle — a big herd. Heading east. And Bill, the Wineglass spread is over there. That herd — shore as hell it's J Bar C cattle, moving in onto the Wineglass range."

Bill Morgan swore softly as his keen old eyes probed the distance. "Right," he growled. "Right as rain, Buck. The J Bar C is moving in on the Wineglass. Jaeger and Cutts are taking the bull by the horns and forcing their luck. This is war, anyway you want to look at it. And if they get that herd in there, it'll be one hell of a job to run 'em out."

He turned, stood in his stirrups and waved a brawny arm. "That dust means J Bar C cattle — moving in on the Wineglass," he yelled. "We got to head 'em off. Come on, boys."

They whipped about, dug in the steel and tore away at a new angle. Once more they dropped down into Coyote Valley, angled up and across it, climbed into the harsh land beyond and drove for the upper reaches of Cotton Valley. They rode silently, grim, intent men on horses which flattened out and ran like scared wolves. And the fury of their pace lifted still another banner of dust against that wide, hot sky which was not missed by the men who were driving that distant herd. And so it was that when Bill Morgan led his men out to where they could see the Wineglass headquarters, they saw also a tight group of riders racing in from the northwest toward the buildings.

Again Bill Morgan waved his arm and gave his wild yell. The men behind him knew what he meant. It was to be a race between them and that other group. Spurs bit deeper. Quirts began to swing. Straining horses responded, while the foam streamed back from outstretched equine jaws.

It was a mad, crazy ride, with the fighting passion of men rising and rising to the exploding point. Buck Comstock, squinting his eyes against the rip of the wind, shouted exultantly, "We got the edge. We're going to beat 'em in!"

Evidently this fact was realized by the other group of riders also, for they whirled to a sudden stop and the sun glittered on rifle barrels as the weapons were dragged from scabbards and levered into action.

The range was long, a good five hundred yards, yet something crackled through the air and told with a fleshy thud. Gus Howard's bronco lunged, staggered, missed its stride and went down, Gus kicking loose from the stirrups and rolling free in the nick of time. He came up roaring mad, jerked his rifle from under the shoulder of the stricken horse and clambering up behind Buck, who had spun his mount to a stop.

"Damn their rotten hearts," yelled Gus in Buck's ear. "They killed the best little parting out bronc that ever packed a kak. Make this goat of yours ramble, Buck. I want to get a cut at those jaspers."

More long range lead whispered savagely by, but Bill Morgan, wise in the ways of battle, roared a command and his men immediately scattered, no longer riding in a compact group, thus making of themselves small, individual targets instead of a massed bulk of men and horses. This strategy carried them safely to the Wineglass headquarters without further casualty to men or horses.

"Find what shelter you can for the broncs," ordered Morgan. "We'll need 'em — later. Bud — take half the men and hole up here around the buildings. Possession, they say, is nine points of the law. Okay — we got possession. We'll keep it. The rest of us will mosey out on foot to meet that crowd. Horses are swell to ride on, but tough to shoot off of, especially with rifles. We can spread out and raise hell with that gang if they try and rush us. Come on."

Rifles in hand, the doughty little group moved away from the ranch buildings, straight toward the first file of cattle, which could now be seen swinging across the wide curve of the upper valley. The riders who had failed in their attempt to beat Morgan and his crowd to the ranch buildings, were still out there, evidently holding council, trying to decide just what to do.

Buck Comstock measured the distance with his eye. "Between six and seven hundred yards, Bill," he shouted. "What say we show 'em we mean business and sort of make up their minds for them?"

"Fair enough," rumbled Morgan. "Try 'em a gun full — everybody."

Rifles lifted, steadied, and began their thin, snarling challenge. Buck Comstock knew a burst of savage joy as his Winchester pounded his shoulder in recoil. At grips with Jaeger and Cutts at last. He swung the lever in smooth cadence and the rifle barrel grew hot under his gripping fingers.

For a moment it seemed as if those ringing volleys were having no effect. Then, abruptly, one of those distant riders threw his hands high and fell backwards from his saddle. And at the same instant a horse began to buck wildly, only to stagger and collapse a moment later. That distant group immediately broke up and whirled away in retreat, heading back to the herd.

Gus Howard yelled exultantly. "You will kill my pet bronc! How do you like some of your own medicine?"

"That's enough," roared Morgan. "Hold your fire. We'll wait a bit, right here."

Bill Morgan, grizzled and wise, had chosen his strategy perfectly. That herd, to get into the heart of the Wineglass range proper, had to pass within a short distance of the ranch buildings. To swing it further east, meant that it would miss the head of Cotton Valley and end up at the fringe of Big Sage Desert. If it worked farther north it would get into the malpais country which spread out from East Butte, clear to the desert. The Wineglass headquarters was the key to the whole thing, a fact Bill Morgan had shrewdly deduced from the very first.

That the J Bar C men also recognized this fact was immediately apparent. Riders dashed out to the point of the herd, halting its progress, circling it, holding the cattle in a compact mass, ready to move in any direction. And still more riders, a good score of them, moved out to meet that first stampeded crowd, to mingle with them and stop well out of range.

The distance was long now, and the heat mirage made it extremely difficult to identify any single object, yet Buck Comstock, watching intently, saw a black horse and a white one, move out from the herd and stop beside that group of undecided riders. Buck felt he knew those horses. They had been seen much together over the Twin Buttes range in the past two years. Jaeger rode the black one, Cutts the white.

"The two he-polecats are out there," yelled Buck. "Jaeger and Cutts are out there."

"I hope they move in a little closer," snarled Gus Howard. "Two or three hundred yards closer. Don't know anything I'd rather do than draw a bead on them two."

"No such good luck, Gus," drawled Johnny Frazier. "Jaeger and Cutts ain't risking their precious hides none. They pay other men to take the real risks."

"Look!" exclaimed Buck. "They're moving out to meet us."

That distant crowd of riders had broken up into little groups and were riding in a wide, circling movement, with the evident intent of surrounding the Wineglass headquarters. It was plainly evident that Jaeger and Cutts were not going to quit without a try for their alley.

Bill Morgan met this move by spreading his defenders in a thin line, all about the ranch buildings. "Get down on your bellies," he told them, as he made the circle and placed each man. "Looks like they intend to rush us. They won't have much chance of tagging you, if you stay flat and close to the ground. If the pressure gets too heavy, give back to the buildings and take cover. Bud and the other boys back there already will be shooting over your heads and give you plenty of help. And make that crowd pay plenty for every inch of ground they take."

Buck Comstock found himself on the north of the ranchhouse. Some seventy-five yards to his left was Johnny Frazier. An equal distance to his right was Gus Howard. Crouched low and peering up ahead of him, Buck saw the same oat topped ridge on which he had been lying when the scream of Jean Harper had brought him to her rescue from Toad Black.

A lot of things had happened since that day. Not so very long ago, either. Yet things had developed, men had died and this whole crisis was moving swiftly toward the inevitable final showdown. It was strange, thought Buck, how little time he had known Jean Harper — and yet how well he knew her. That was the way with life when it was stirred from its usual placid pace. Two people, fighting side by side for a scant half hour, would know each other better in that time than they would in a year of casual acquaintance. Passion, conflict, fury — these things speeded up the tempo and developments of life incredibly. Buck wrenched his thoughts from Jean Harper, to the more deadly problem ahead.

A man, he mused, coming over the top of that ridge on a horse, would sure make a fat target against the sky. He spread a fan of yellow cartridges on the ground beside him, cracked the action of his rifle to make sure it was ready to go, then settled back into tense waiting.

The J Bar C force had cut over that ridge, well back to the north, and for some time all was quiet and nothing in sight. Buck lifted his head slightly and looked over at Johnny Frazier, who caught the look and waved gaily. Johnny, thought Buck, was one swell guy, in a fight or out of one. Long, lean and coolly drawing, Johnny would do to ride the river with, any old time. Good natured and slow to anger, but a buzzsaw on wheels when he did get his roach set. A man who would go all the way for a friend.

And Gus Howard, over there on the other side of him. Gus was a hard boiled fighting man, any way you looked at him. He'd go through, Gus would. A man could not ask two more staunch scrappers to help him hold down a piece of country.

Well over on the west of the buildings a lone rifle snarled. It seemed to be a signal, for the voice of it was picked up and swelled to a roar. Buck, unconsciously twisting his head to see what was going on over there, was brought abruptly to matters out in front of him, when a bullet chugged savagely into the ground not a foot from his head, spattering him with bits of earth.

He ducked, his slitted eyes searching along the rim above him. Up there a man was kneeling, gun trained, so it seemed to Buck, dead on him. Buck snapped his own rifle up, but before he could get it into line, Johnny Frazier's rifle crashed out over on his left. That kneeling figure on the ridge seemed to turn a complete back somersault.

From the corner of his eye Buck saw the peak of a sombrero lifting into sight in that fringe of oats against the skyline. His rifle settled to his shoulder, the sights steadied and the gun slammed back in recoil. The sombrero disappeared abruptly. Yet the thin, wicked lashing of smokeless powder along the top of the ridge grew in volume.

Buck, his eyes straining warily to pick up another target, could hear lead hissing past him, most of it well above as it seemed to be reaching for the ranch buildings behind. But soon some of it began chugging into the earth about him once more and he knew that another sharpshooter up on the ridge was working at him.

Sounded a muffled, metallic clash and Buck felt a quick, twisting jerk of his left foot and ankle. For a moment he thought he'd been hit, then realized that a speeding slug had split itself on his jutting spur rowel. Buck tried to flatten himself deeper into the hard, sun-baked earth, swearing softly between set teeth because he could not get sight of a target.

For a moment lead ceased to pound around him and Buck looked to his left, just in time to see Johnny Frazier cut loose another shot. He looked to the right, where Gus Howard had pulled up high on his elbows to work the lever of his rifle.

Buck distinctly saw Gus cringe as a slug told with a fleshy clout. He saw the tense life in Gus' arms and shoulders flow out of them, saw the half opened rifle drop from

Gus' hands. He saw the stricken man's head roll forward and drop. And then Gus Howard looked just like a bundle of clothes, tossed aside.

A chill went over Buck Comstock, a chill which turned instantly to a hot, blind fury. Gus Howard was dead. Buck knew that. Even a mortally wounded man, while life still exists in him, has substance. But there was no substance to Gus Howard — now. He was just a flattened, shrunken bundle of clothes spilled lifelessly on the ground.

Buck lurched to his knees, to his feet, a hoarse feral cry of fury in the throat of him. Something seemed to have snapped in the brain of him. He had gone berserk. He started up that slope, running. Buck's ears registered a dim shouting, but it made no impression on him. He did not know that it was Johnny Frazier, aghast at Buck's lone, reckless, wild charge, howling at him to get down, to get close to the safety of the earth. And when Buck did not heed nor slow up a step, Johnny reared up and raced after him.

Out back, there in the ranch buildings, Bud Tharp began to curse brokenly as he saw those wild two, apparently gone completely loco, dashing up that slope toward the hungry guns on top of it. Bud did the only thing he could to help out. He bawled orders to the men about him, pointed to Buck and Johnny, and threw up his own rifle. The punchers understood. They began lacing the top of that ridge with a hurricane of lead, laying down a virtual barrage ahead of that reckless pair.

Yet, all too soon Buck and Johnny were so close to the top of the ridge, the men in back of them had to slacken their fire to keep from hitting them. Buck, oblivious to all except the savage fury in him, surged clear of the top of the ridge. He wanted to come up against the renegade who had killed Gus Howard — he wanted that hombre right in front of him, where he could blast him with gunflame and lead and burn him down.

A swarthy, savage-eyed figure lurched into sight, moving in a crouching run along the far side of the ridge, just low enough down to keep under the hail of lead which had lashed the ridge top a moment before. At the same instant he and Buck saw each other and it was a duel of speed as to which could throw down and shoot the quickest. Maybe the fellow was surprised, a little bewildered at finding an enemy right there in front of him. At any rate Buck gained a heartbeat of time as he snapped at his target like he might have at a running deer. The swarthy one spun around and dropped. The next instant something crashed against the back of Buck's legs, knocking him sprawling.

That something was Johnny Frazier's body and Johnny rolled right on up to the small of Buck's back to hold him down. "You raving, wild-eyed lunatic," panted Johnny. "Stay flat before I larrup you with a gun barrel. What the hell got into you? Do you want to get us both killed?"

Buck struggled to get free. "They killed Gus Howard," he gulped hoarsely. "They killed Gus, I tell you. I saw the bullet hit him — and the way he flattened out — God — !"

"Getting both of us killed won't help Gus now," growled the practical Johnny. "You can't lick that whole gang single handed. Stay down there, you spavin-brained tarantula bug. Promise to stay down or I hold you here until you grow whiskers."

Buck's brain was clearing of his first wild fury. He dropped his head against one outstretched forearm, and nodded. "Okay, Johnny — I'm cooled off some, now."

Johnny slithered out beside Buck. "You watch south, I'll watch north," he said.

"We lather these jaspers on the flank and they'll hightail it in a hurry."

Buck lifted himself high enough in the wild oats to look south along the ridge. He could not see anyone, but just for luck he searched the waving, sun dried grass with three or four slugs. This unexpected barrage from the flank brought a startled, wild-eyed rider into view, who popped from the grass like a jumped coyote. The fellow seemed to understand the situation at a glance, for he made no attempt whatever at fighting back. Instead, he angled down the east slope of the ridge at a dead run, tearing for a group of ground reined horses in the hollow.

It would have been simple enough to have knocked him over, but of a sudden, Buck had no stomach for any more killing. After all, that fleeing puncher wasn't Jaeger or Cutts. He was just another cowboy, riding and fighting for his hire. Under different circumstances he might have been a good friend. So Buck contented himself with merely dusting those flying bootheels with whistling lead, an experiment which brought an amazing burst of speed from the sprinting puncher.

Into the midst of the horses dodged the puncher, to pop immediately into a saddle and swing out to the east at a dead run. Farther down the ridge someone was yelling wildly. Then, from various points four more men appeared, racing for the horses. They, like the first, Buck allowed to reach their broncos and spur away.

Panic is an insidious thing, stampeding even the most valiant of men at times. Convinced by the sight of their fleeing comrade that something was decidedly wrong on this particular ridge, the attackers cleared out in a hurry, swinging beyond rifle range and circling back toward the cattle herd, well to the north.

Things grew quiet along the ridge. There were still three horses left down there in that hollow. Buck's brain was working logically again. That kneeling man Johnny Frazier had first cut down — that sombrero he himself had driven a bullet through — and that other huddled figure down below — the swarthy one. Three men — and three riderless horses. The account was pretty well squared for Gus Howard.

Johnny Frazier came over to Buck. "Kinda looks like things had fallen apart on this side," he drawled.

Buck nodded. "They scared easier than I thought they would."

Johnny looped his rifle under one arm and built a cigarette. "Those jaspers are only fighting for wages," he said. "We're fighting for our range. That makes a difference, Buck."

A survey of the situation on all sides showed that the attack had broken up. Gun fire had died to only a few last sporadic reports, long range shots carrying an expression of defiance or hate, rather than any hope of hitting. Buck and Johnny, from the elevation of the ridge, could see the J Bar C forces circling wide of the ranch buildings and drifting back to the herd. There was more than one empty saddle among them.

"The party," drawled Johnny, "seems to be over. Mister Jaeger and Mister Cutts seem to have burned their fingers. But they made a fool play in the first place, trying to rush this ranch with all the boys holed up and ready for them. I reckon they been so used to seeing folks cave in front of them, they couldn't figure there's plenty of men on this range who can look 'em right in the eye and jam a slug between their molars."

Buck nodded. "Let's go down and get Gus."

They carried the body of Gus Howard into the ranch buildings, where grim, hard eyed men came out to meet them, Bud

Tharp in the lead. Bud asked no question, for he had eyes to see. "A good man," he said softly. "We'll all miss him."

"Any more — get it?" asked Johnny.

"Tim Donovan is pretty hard hit. I'm afraid for him. Jigger Lewis has a smashed arm and Porky Powers got nicked in the shoulder. Bill Morgan has a broken leg."

Bud had a smear of blood along the angle of his jaw. "They didn't miss you more than a mile," said Johnny Frazier.

Bud felt his jaw, looked at his hand, shrugged. "Come on — we got work to do."

While they were checking up and caring for their wounded, Tim Donovan died. The others were not too seriously wounded, providing they got a doctor's care reasonably soon. Bill Morgan was cussing the pain of his wounded leg. But Tharp sent out a couple of punchers to scout the future moves of the J Bar C.

Buck Comstock went over to Bill Morgan. "This," said Morgan harshly, touching his wounded leg — "sorta makes me of little use with this star. Who'll put it on next, Buck?"

"That's easy," said Bud Tharp. "Here — gimme it."

Bud took the star, turned and pinned it

on Buck. "What you say, goes, Buck. We'll follow you to hell and gone."

"Correct," chimed in Johnny Frazier. "Only," he added, grinning — "I might renege on that last if you go charging blind up any more hills, like you did out there today. I'll tell a man I aged one hell of a lot, chasing you up that ridge. I died about thirty times and was plumb surprised to find I was still alive and all in one piece when I hit the top."

"Fair enough," said Buck soberly. "I won't make any more fool breaks like that one. There ain't much to figure out. The issue is straight up and down. The quicker I can settle it, the less good men will have to die. I'm going after Jaeger and Cutts."

The scouts whom Bud Tharp had sent out, came back to report that the J Bar C herd had been turned and was driving back the way it had come.

"Maybe they mean it — maybe it is only a bluff," said Buck. "Either way, we play our cards carefully. The wounded will head for the Circle Star. Doc Pollard will probably still be there, looking after Brood Shotwell. The rest of us will follow that herd and make sure it isn't a bluff. After that — Jaeger and Cutts. I'll put 'em in their graves — or behind bars — if it is the last thing I ever do."

Bill Morgan, Jigger Lewis and Porky Powers, rudely bandaged, were helped into their saddles. "Think you can make it, Bill?" asked Buck anxiously.

"Hell, yes," Morgan snorted. "I ain't as young as I used to be, but it'll take more than a smashed leg to put me all the way down. And listen, kid — don't get too reckless. The way things are shaping up now, we got a definite edge on that pair of whelps. Their plans have gone sour in a dozen different places. Instead of catching us by surprise as they first figured, it turned out the other way around. We're wised up and on the fight. They're getting desperate and panicky. Else they never would have tried such a rattle weeded trick as they did today. Play your cards careful and slow. There won't be any satisfaction for Bud and Johnny and me and the rest in winning, if you go get yourself killed. Was I you, I'd let those jaspers stew in their own juice for a time, while I went to work and gathered up a few loose ends and found out where they led to."

"What you driving at?" Buck frowned.

"Who killed Judge Henning — and why, for one," said Morgan. "And why did St. Ives shoot Brood Shotwell in the back?"

"I think I can answer that one now," said Buck, his eyes narrowing. "St. Ives was just another rat bought up by J Bar C money. He knew that Jean Harper was held at the Stirrup Cross and when he realized that Brood Shotwell was going to search the place and be certain to find her, he shot him in the back. That is the way it looks to me. Well, you get along and have that leg taken care of. I'll try and keep a level head on my shoulders, Bill."

"See that you do that," growled Morgan. "Don't go charging up any more ridges with the idea of licking the whole damned world single-handed. You may be a lot of man, kid — but there are limits. Damn this leg. It hurts like billy-hell."

The three wounded men rode off on their way to the Circle Star. At the Wineglass there ensued a period of grim faced labor with pick and shovel. Then Buck took Johnny Frazier and Bud Tharp aside and asked their opinions.

"I think Bill was right," said Bud Tharp. "If we go pile-driving in on this outfit, there'll be a lot of us where Gus and Tim are now. The sane, sensible play is to work around cagey like until we can snap up Jaeger and Cutts, if possible without getting tangled up in a brawl with their crew.

Without leaders the J Bar C crew won't fight, that's a cinch. And without having to lick that crew, we'll keep good men alive. I agree with Bill. Let's use our heads first and then our guns if we have to."

"We'll try it," agreed Buck. "We'll take the boys left here with us and follow that herd. The afternoon is about gone. We'll stick behind that herd until dark. If they keep it moving it will be just about back on the J Bar C range by then. And they won't be able to stir those cow critters up enough to get 'em back here through the dark and everything before tomorrow morning. Soon as we're sure of the herd, we'll cut back to the Circle Star and get some rest and grub. Tomorrow morning early, I'll send two or three of the boys up here to keep watch and see that the J Bar C doesn't try and slide a herd in here again. For myself, I'll head for town in the morning and lay around there a bit and wait for that chance at Jaeger and Cutts in person. Come on."

Tired, hungry and grim, Buck led his little force of top fighting men back to the Circle Star some two hours after dark. Weary broncos were turned into the cavvy corral and Bones Baker worked overtime feeding hungry men. As soon as he had washed up and eaten, Buck went down to the bunkhouse, where he found the wounded resting easily under the care of Doc Pollard.

Doc looked Buck over with twinkling eyes. "I'll be going on strike pretty quick, young fellow. Never was so overworked in my life before. When is this sort of thing going to stop?"

"I shore hope you won't have another case, Doc," answered Buck soberly. "But you can charge up all this to Jaeger and Cutts. They're raising hell all across this range."

"I know," agreed Doc thoughtfully. "A pair of bad eggs, those two. Walk carefully, Buck. They're clever, even if they are first class coyotes."

"How's Brood making it?"

"Doing very well indeed. Miss Harper is up looking after him."

From the bunkhouse, Buck went up to the main house, where Shotwell had been first taken. He went in quietly, moving on his tiptoes. A low turned lamp was burning in the sick room, and a slim figure sat quietly beside the wounded man's bed. As she saw Buck's tall, lean figure in the doorway, she came to him quickly and silently, pushed him out and closed the door.

"It's wonderful, Buck," she murmured. "I don't see how he does it, wounded so terribly. But honestly — I think he's going to get well. The strength of his heart is amazing, but he must be kept absolutely quiet."

Buck was filled with a queer, poignant yearning. This girl, so deft and quiet and swift. Just a dim shadow there beside him, looking up at him.

"I'm mighty glad of the good news," mumbled Buck. "Brood is a good man — a mighty good man. I know you'll take good care of him. I'll be glad when this range is healthy again. I — I got some serious things to talk to you about, Jean."

He couldn't read her expression. It was too dark, there in the hall. She was very, very still. Then her voice came to him, little more than a murmur. "I — I'll be glad to hear those things — Buck."

Then, before he could stop her, she had dodged into the sick room again and the door closed once more. Traveling on his tiptoes, Buck stole away.

CHAPTER TWELVE

The next day at a little past noon, Buck Comstock and Johnny Frazier rode in to Twin Buttes. The town seemed a trifle busier than usual, for this time of day. Quite a number of saddle animals were lined along the hitch rails. "Some of the J Bar C crowd in town," drawled Johnny softly.

Buck nodded. "We'll look around," he said briefly, reining in and dismounting before Pete Allen's store. They went in and found Pete Allen alone, a stocky, powerfully built man with a square jaw, bristling hair and direct, shrewd eyes. He stared at Buck in patent amazement.

"Well," he said slowly — "I'll be eternally damned."

Buck smiled briefly. "I reckon it does sort of surprise you, Pete — to see me here, wearing Brood Shotwell's star."

"Surprised," ejaculated Allen — "is hardly the word. Plumb flabbergasted is closer to it."

"There's a story behind it all, Pete," said Buck.

"There must be — there shore must be. Where the hell is Brood — and where is Spike St. Ives — and what's going on out on the range that's keeping Doc Pollard? There's a lot of damn funny things going on around here that's got a lot of us fighting our heads. Hear somebody put a slug through Judge Henning. Not two hours ago Buss Shugrue got the shock of a lifetime. He went to the livery barn barley bin to do a little feeding and when he opened the bin what did he find? I'll tell you what he found — he found Duke Younger in that bin, dead as a mackerel. He'd had his skull knocked in with a gun-butt. This damned stretch of country has gone nuts."

Buck looked at Johnny Frazier. "That's news aplenty, Pete — about Younger, I mean," he said. "Who, I wonder, would have killed him?"

"Don't ask me. I tell you I'm plenty spooked the way things are going," growled Allen. "And you still ain't told me how you, a fugitive from justice, is waltzing around free and easy and wearing the star of the man supposed to be out looking for you."

Buck looked Allen straight in the eye. "Pete you're square — and sensible. Here's the story." He told then of the dastardly attempt on Brood Shotwell's life by Spike St. Ives, and of the abrupt finish of St. Ives. He told of the attempt of the J Bar C to take over the Wineglass and throw a herd of J Bar C cattle onto the Wineglass range. He told of finding Jean Harper held prisoner on the Stirrup Cross and her story of abduction by Leek Jaeger and Frank Cutts. He told of the confession of Duke Younger and Toad Black that the jury had been bought. "All of that, Pete — is why I'm here, wearing this star. St. Ives is dead and Brood Shotwell bad wounded. Somebody has to represent the law, with hell breaking loose the way it is. Bill Morgan started out to wear this star, but he got a smashed leg in the brawl out at the Wineglass. So he moved the star on to me. All this is going to set a lot of people back on their heels, Pete — but they'll have to take it and like it. I'm packing this star now and I aim to make the authority stick."

"There'll be some who'll question that authority — from you, Buck," said Pete Allen gravely.

"Do you?"

"No. I never was satisfied the way you

were treated in that trial. I know several folks who feel the same way. It won't be us you'll have to worry about. But Jaeger and Cutts will buck plenty."

"I expect them to," nodded Buck. "It won't do 'em any good though. Pete, back of all the hell on this range stand Jaeger and Cutts. Think over all I've told you and see if you don't see the same picture."

A shadow darkened the store doorway and the maker of it, squinting into the gloom, came a few steps in. It was Rope Tenny, one of the J Bar C punchers. Of a sudden he froze. He had recognized Buck Comstock. His breath gave out in a startled hiss. He whirled toward the door.

"Hold it, Tenny," rasped Buck. "I got a gun on you!"

"And I'm backing Buck's play — all the way, Rope," cut in Johnny Frazier.

Tenny halted, his hands lifting slightly. "What yuh want with me?" he growled. "I ain't done a thing."

"No," drawled Buck. "But you would have. Come over here."

Tenny came and Johnny Frazier, at a nod from Buck, took Tenny's gun. "Who," demanded Buck — "is over in the Yellow Horse?"

Tenny shrugged. "Just a few of the gang."

"Are Jaeger and Cutts there?"

"No."

"Will they be there, any time today?"

"Mebbe — mebbe not," growled Tenny. "I don't know what their plans are."

"Keep your eye on him, Johnny," said Buck. "I want to take a look see."

He moved up at an angle to the door and peered out. Over there across the street, grouped about the door of the Yellow Horse, were nearly a dozen riders and the eyes of all of them were on the store. In the forefront of the crowd stood a wiry, compact man, carrying two guns slung low and tied down. Even at that distance a livid, ugly scar across the man's face was visible. A chill flicker ran up and down Buck's spine, an instinctive bristling of antagonism. That man with the two tied down guns was Whistler Hahn!

Buck turned back into the store, shot out a long arm and caught Rope Tenny by the slack of his shirt. "They sent you over here — to find out — what?" he growled.

"Nobody sent me," blurted Tenny. "I came over here to get some smoking."

"That's a lie! You can buy Durham in the Yellow Horse. There's a dozen men over there, with Whistler Hahn in front of them, watching this store. Untangle that crooked tongue of yours and give me the straight of this. Or —"

Tenny licked his lips. "I was to find out who was with Frazier," he admitted. "Nobody saw you two jaspers ride in, but one of the boys spotted that claybank of Frazier's. They didn't recognize the other bronc and they wondered who was with him. That — that's all I know."

Buck pushed him away, went back to the door. Whistler Hahn was haranguing that group of riders in front of the Yellow Horse. Abruptly the group split up, some going up the street, some down. Hahn with three others, started across the street toward the store.

"We're in for it, Johnny," said Buck over his shoulder. "Tie Tenny up — fast. Pete, your store may get some holes shot in it."

"Fair enough," said Pete Allen calmly. "Close the door if you want to, Buck."

"Not yet. Maybe in a minute or two. How's your back door?"

"I'm going to lock it right now."

"Watch that Hahn jasper close, Buck," warned Johnny Frazier. "He didn't get his reputation because he was slow on the draw. Quiet down there, Tenny — or I'll bend a gun over your head."

Buck drew both belt guns and poised

himself just off the flare of daylight which came in the open door. A moment later his voice rang out, cold and crisp. "Far enough, Hahn. What's eatin' you?"

Outside Whistler Hahn stopped, as did the three men behind him. His thumbs hooked in his gun belts. His scarred, pointed face seemed to jut from under the brim of his hat. "We're lookin' for Rope Tenny," he said, his words carrying that sibilant, whistling note. "He in there?"

"He's in here," answered Buck — "and staying here. Anything else?"

"Yeah. Who in hell are you?"

"I know," cried one of the men with Hahn. "I know that voice. It's Buck Comstock!"

Buck knew the game was up now. He leaped to the heavy, sliding door, threw his weight against it. The door slid closed with a bang and Pete Allen, appearing from nowhere, threw the heavy, locking hasp into place.

Outside sounded a volley of shrill, whistling curses, then a thudding roll of gunfire. Lead socked into the door, came through, peeling back big, white splinters. The two front windows, one on either side of the door, small and high up, dropped shattered glass as lead cut through them.

Long, pealing yells echoed over the town. There was a sinister something in those yells, much as though a wolf pack was gathering for the kill.

Johnny Frazier, finished with the task of tying up Rope Tenny, came over beside Buck. "This," he drawled, "looks interestin'."

Buck nodded. "It's tough on Pete, though. I was a damn fool to come here in the first place."

"Don't worry about me or the store," said Pete Allen quietly. "I ain't altogether blind. I've seen a showdown coming up for a long time between the J Bar C and the rest of the Twin Buttes range. Until it broke it was none of my business. Now that it has I've got to take sides. All the time I knew there was only one side for me. That's the side I'm on now. I'll see your crowd through, Buck."

"That's white of you, Pete. When this is over, our side won't forget."

At that moment there sounded several heavy blows at the back of the store. "They're working on the back door," exclaimed Pete. "I'll discourage that, pronto."

He grabbed a six-shooter from under his counter and ran to the rear of the place, back where the shadows were deep and thick and piles of merchandise filled the gloom. The next moment the confines of the store shuddered under the rolling snarl of several shots. Outside rose a howl of pain, then a string of bawling, furious curses.

"I gave 'em a gun full," yelled Pete Allen. "They won't get so close to that door again."

Answering lead crashed through the back door and Allen, with Johnny Frazier's help, quickly threw up a barricade of sacked flour. "Let 'em shoot and be damned now," panted Allen. "They won't get far."

Out in front things had quieted somewhat. Then came the challenge of Whistler Hahn's voice. "Listen to gospel, Allen. Turn Frazier and Comstock out here or it'll be the worse for you. If you want your store left in one piece — turn 'em out. I mean it!"

"I stick to my friends, Hahn," Allen answered him. "And you're not one of them."

Again came that burst of furious, sibilant cursing and another volley of lead into the heavy front door. "I reckon," said Johnny Frazier, drawing a gun and moving over to one of the front windows — "I reckon we might as well start shootin' for keeps. If we could get that wolf of a Hahn down, it might take a lot out of that crowd. Me for the try, anyhow."

"Take it easy," warned Buck. "They'll be watchin' those windows."

Johnny flattened against the wall, tipped his gun over the sill and started to rise up for a quick snapshot. The next moment a livid stream of sparks bloomed and Johnny's gun was smashed from his grip and to the floor. Johnny whirled away from the window, gripping his right hand and swearing savagely.

"Get you, boy?" cried Buck anxiously. "Did they get you?"

"No," rasped Johnny. "But they shot my gun out of my hand. My arm feels paralyzed, clear to the shoulder."

"Let me look."

In the dim light Buck examined Johnny's hand. There was new blood on it, but Buck saw with relief that the blood came from shallow surface cuts where the lead of the speeding slug had spattered. There was a slight cut on Johnny's jaw, also from spattered lead and also bleeding.

Now another slug came through that same window and slogged into a barrel of dried apricots, not far from the door. Outside a rifle clanged thinly.

"Thought so," exclaimed Pete Allen. "Somebody is up high, shootin' down through that window. The slug that hit your gun, Johnny — came from a rifle. I could tell by the report."

Buck glanced from apricot barrel to window, judging the angle. "Break me out a new rifle, Pete," he ordered. "Wipe the grease out of it and bring it here with some cartridges."

The firing outside had dwindled off somewhat and at that moment sounded the tattoo of speeding hoofs. Buck sought the safer window and took a quick look. "Jaeger and Cutts," he exclaimed. "With six or eight more men. Now we do catch hell, boys."

"Here's your rifle," said Pete Allen, thrusting the weapon into Buck's hand. "And it's loaded."

Again Buck judged the angle from the right hand window to apricot barrel. He nodded, moving to the left hand window and back a trifle from it. There, by standing upright, he could look across the street and see the high false front above the Yellow Horse. And he muttered in satisfaction.

He could see the enemy rifleman now.

The fellow was standing on some sort of support behind the false front of the Yellow Horse, with head and shoulders visible, a rifle cuddled to his face. Even as Buck looked that rifle leaped in recoil and another whistling bullet came through the right hand window and slammed the floor near the barrel.

Buck did not hesitate. Time for any squeamishness was long since past. This was dog eat dog. His own rifle spat flame and ringing report. It was as though a gust of hurricane wind had struck that man on the false front across the street. He was whipped back from his perch and Buck distinctly heard the crash of his fall as he struck the roof of the Yellow Horse. A moment later he came into view again, rolling down the slant of the roof and plummeting to the ground, where he lay a huddled heap.

"They want hell," growled Buck savagely. "They can have it!"

The killing of their sharpshooter brought a reaction of curses and angry yells and then a hail of lead, ripping through both windows and both doors. The store was full of invisible, whispering droning things of death. A ricocheting slug slammed into a shelf of "air tights," bringing several of the cans down with a clatter.

"I'm sorry, Pete," said Buck. "They're going to make a mess out of this store."

"Sorry, be damned!" snorted Pete. "I'm not sorry. I'm mad — plenty. Just because they want to get hold of you is no excuse for that gang to shoot my store all to hell and gone. It's high time Jaeger and Cutts and their crowd got their ears knocked down and I'm aiming to sit into this thing until that time comes. Don't you worry none about my store. I'll take the pay for all damage out of their cussed hides. I'm going to break out my old scatter gun."

Buck and Johnny made no attempt to answer the shooting. They crouched aside, well out of line and let the slugs drive past. If the hostile force did nothing more than shoot through door and window they never would get any results.

As though realization of this came to the attackers, the fire dwindled and died. Pete Allen came sliding over beside Buck. He had a double-barreled shotgun in his hands. "I ain't got a load of buckshot in the joint," he complained disgustedly. "I got some ordered but they ain't showed up yet. I got a lot of quail loads though, and at close range they'll discourage some of those bimbos — plenty."

Outside came a shout. It was Leek Jaeger and he addressed his remarks to Pete Allen. "We want Comstock," bawled Jaeger. "We're going to get him, one way or another. Better listen to reason, Allen. If you want any store left, run Comstock out of there. You won't get another chance."

"If he's in the open," growled Pete — "I'll answer him."

The doughty storekeeper slipped over to a window, stood on his tiptoes and looked out. Instantly his shotgun leaped to his shoulder and roared. From the far side of the street sounded a shriek of pain and surprise. Pete Allen came back to Buck and Johnny, laughing softly.

"It was Jaeger," he chuckled. "He had turned to talk to somebody in the Yellow Horse and I sure lathered his britches with bird shot. I shore woke him up and he hit for shelter lickety-larrup."

There came another flurry of shots and then another period of silence. This stillness lasted so long it became ominous. Buck prowled to a window, took a quick survey. "Nobody in sight," he announced. "But they're figuring up some deviltry. I can feel it."

"Maybe getting ready for a big rush,"

drawled Johnny. "That's their only chance and they'll get around to realizing it before long."

As if in answer to this sage observation, the whole store building shook under the impact of a terrific crash. Wood splintered and metal hinges squealed in protest. It was as though a sudden gust of heavy wind swept through the store.

"The back door," yelled Buck. "They've rammed it in!"

A bellow of triumphant yells affirmed this. And at this moment another hail of lead smashed into the front of the store. It was Pete Allen and his scatter gun who saved the moment. He leaped to one side, so that he could see back the length of the store. There the splintered, unhinged door, transfixed on the end of a heavy timber which had served the attackers as a battering ram, lay crookedly across the barricade of sacked flour which Pete had thrown up. And through the opening beyond, a group of men were crowding and fighting their way. Once that group got inside the store, the answer would be quick. Pete Allen swung up his scatter gun and drove two loads of birdshot into the midst of them.

That hail of fine shot was not fatal, but it

was painful and blinding and disconcerting. The charge broke and the men scattered, their frenzied cursing a horrid aftermath of the sullen bellow of the shotgun. But the respite offered was of short duration. Through that shattered door now came a sleet of lead, fanning up and down, right and left. Johnny Frazier gasped, reeled and went down.

Instantly Buck Comstock was on his knees beside his stricken friend. "Johnny! Johnny! God — man — where did they get you?"

But Johnny did not answer. His head, as Buck tried to lift it, lolled limply from side to side. Down one side of it, staining Buck's lifting fingers, was a thickening fan of blood.

Buck went cold all over. His eyes seemed to sink into his head and the muscles of his face tautened until his profile was bony and rigid. He rose to his feet, caught up his rifle, started for that back door.

"Watch the front, Pete," he rasped.

The shooting through the rear door stopped. There sounded a rush of booted feet and again the opening was jammed with charging men. Into the very center of that mass Buck levered his rifle empty, grabbed it by the barrel and hurled it after the lead it had thrown. Then he whipped out both belt guns and began rolling them.

No matter what its cause, human anger and courage could not stand up against such a deadly fusillade. Dead men slumped limply down. Wounded men fell on top of them. Others, who by some miracle had escaped that merciless lead, fought their way free of the shambles and rushed away, terror stricken.

Mechanically Buck Comstock punched the empty shells from his guns, thumbed fresh loads into the cylinders, then started for that open door. He was through skulking under cover, through with situations which had brought death to his friends. First Gus Howard. Then Tim Donovan. Now — Johnny Frazier — good old Johnny Frazier. And there was Jigger Lewis and Bill Morgan and Porky Powers wounded. While he, who was really the crux of the whole set-up, was still untouched.

Yes, he was done with skulking. He was going out after Leek Jaeger and Frank Cutts and he was going to jam hot lead through them when he found them.

Behind Buck, Pete Allen was yelling at him, begging him to wait, begging him not to go out. But Buck never heard him. He stalked to that rear door, climbed over the tangle of dead and dying men and swung around the back of the store to the alley way and ran between the store and the hotel.

It did not strike him as strange that there were none left back there to roll smoke with. He had blown that charge at the back door to pieces, hadn't he? He'd sent those J Bar C coyotes running for cover, hadn't he? Well, he'd go out front now and repeat the dose.

He went up the alley, a tall, lean figure, leaning slightly forward as though he was following the trail of some stampeded quarry. There was no expression of his jutting, tight-locked profile. And his eyes, far back in his head burned like feverish coals.

And then, when he was less than a dozen steps from the end of the alley, two men swung into it from the street. Recognition was instantaneous. Those two were Leek Jaeger and Whistler Hahn!

The advantage of surprise lay with Buck. He was strung tight to a state of cold, rigid, mechanical purpose. He was beyond a state where anything might surprise or upset him. On the other hand, Buck Comstock was the last person in the world whom Jaeger and Hahn would expect to find marching up the alley toward them.

Buck threw his first shot at Whistler Hahn, almost a though his subconscious self had analyzed the situation and decided that Hahn was the more dangerous of the two. The lead went home somewhere, for Hahn spun around, staggered and leaned against the outer wall of the store for support. But he did not go down and he whipped out one gun and began to shoot.

Buck minded that shooting not one whit. His blazing eyes were on Leek Jaeger's stumpy figure now and he was throwing lead at the man, as much as he would have thrown his fists, with an unconscious hunching of his shoulder at each shot and a low, panting, huh — huh — huh, as though he was driving that lead home with physical as well as mechanical force.

Jaeger had started for his guns, but got neither of them out of the leather. Buck's first slug took him deep in the body and Jaeger began to reel backward, his hands thrown up before his face as though he would ward off some dread spectre. Then he began to sag, and suddenly he halted in his backward stagger, rocked forward on his toes and pitched out on his face.

At that moment something struck Buck a terrific blow in the chest. It sent him reeling the entire width of the alley. His knees began to sag under him, but somehow he kept himself erect, his burning eyes whipping over to Whistler Hahn. The gunman no longer sagged against the side of the store. He had slid down until he was half lying, half sitting on the ground. Hahn's rodent teeth were bared in a set snarl and his eyes were a weasel red. He was trying to set a wavering gun on a line with Buck's heart.

Buck shot twice, mechanically. Hahn's head jerked back and he flattened out in a twisted, awkward heap. Buck staggered and went down on one knee.

For a time he stayed there. There was a livid fire burning in his chest now and a deathly weakness gripped at his vitals. A haze was gathering before his eyes and he shook his head savagely in a effort to clear his vision.

Slowly he got back to his feet. The job wasn't over with yet. Frank Cutts still remained — and he had to get Cutts! He had to wipe out the last of that ratnest. He had to get Cutts!

He took a step — he took another. He went up the alley to the street in staggering lurches, like a man in the last dregs of drunkenness. This alley, which had always seemed reasonably level before had suddenly become filled with dips and ridges and hollows — things to stumble over. And that agony in his chest was spreading now, up to his throat, down into his hips, while his legs were growing numb.

Suddenly the alley was gone and he was in the lone street of Twin Buttes. There was a roaring in his ears, a rapidly growing thunder. Up the street came a madly riding bunch of men. And was it that damned haze before his eyes which was tricking him or was that really Bud Tharp riding at the head of that charging group of riders? Damn that haze. He hadn't realized it was so late. The sun must have gone down. It sure as hell was getting dark.

Over across the street, in the doorway of the Yellow Horse, a single shot blared. Another terrific force struck Buck Comstock, this time high in the right shoulder. The impact spun him around and his knees gave way entirely this time. He felt the impact of the ground striking him, like it was a far away, entirely irrelevant thing. And then blackness swooped down upon him, gulping him up, carrying him away and away —.

And so it was that Buck did not see Bud Tharp, shooting from the saddle at a wild riding speed, cut down on Frank Cutts as the latter stood in the doorway of the Yellow Horse, just in the act of levering another cartridge into the chamber of the rifle he held.

But Tharp never made a better shot. The .45 slug took Cutts just above the left eye and Cutts crumpled where he stood, the whole back of his head blown out.

CHAPTER THIRTEEN

Buck Comstock had the feeling that he had been away on a long, long journey, before coming back to the world of men. He had to climb up and up from immeasurable depths, through pits filled with all kinds of grisly horrors. Yet, eventually he reached the top of that pit and floated away on soft, white restful clouds, clouds that were so smooth and restful a guy could sleep and sleep and sleep.

However, even on this haven of clouds, every so often there were devils who followed him from the pit to stick their damned fingers into his chest and shoulder, hurting him like all get out. He tried to cuss those devils, plenty, but somehow it was just too much trouble and effort. So he got to waiting patiently until the devils left him and he could go back to sleep again.

Came a day when bright, living warmth lay on his face and made him open his eyes. He blinked painfully. He sure must have been asleep a mighty long time to have the light hurt his eyes the way it did. He tried to puzzle it all out and, puzzling, made a startling discovery. It was the sun, good old sun, that made the brightness and warmth. Good old sun! Buck sighed, grinned ecstatically and then, exhausted by thought and discovery, went back to sleep again.

His strength came back fast, after that. The devils had gone back to the pit for good. They did not come out to plague him any more, nor to jab their devilish fingers into his chest and shoulder like they used to. And one fine morning Buck discovered that it wasn't white clouds he was resting on, but clean white sheets instead. Hell! He was in bed!

This discovery seemed to set a new and vigorous tide of strength sweeping through him. He looked all around him, as far as an amazingly heavy head would permit in turning. Off to one side he discovered another bed and on it was Johnny Frazier. Johnny had a big white bandage about his head and was sitting up, propped against some pillows, reading a lop-eared magazine.

"Hi!" whispered Buck weakly. "Hi, you

old leather pounder. How's things?"

Johnny's bandaged head jerked around and a look of keen pleasure swept over his face. He grinned. "Hi, yourself, old thunderbug. How you feeling?"

"Hungry," whispered Buck. "Hungry as hell. Don't they ever feed a man around this damned spread?"

Before Johnny could answer a door creaked slightly as it opened. Through that door came Doc Pollard — and Jean Harper, who looked prettier than any girl had a right to be, in starched, spotless gingham. Johnny nodded toward Buck.

"He's awake at last, Doc. And hungry."

"Fine!" effused Doc heartily. "Fine! Hungry, eh? That means he's got his feet back on the trail."

Both Doc and Jean Harper came over and stood beside Buck's bed. Doc's grin was one of professional exultance over still once again giving a licking to the old man with the reaper. But the smile on Jean Harper's lips was one of tremulous gentleness and there was a softly brooding look in her dark eyes. Johnny Frazier, marking that look, smiled to himself and dug deep into his magazine.

"So you want something to eat, eh?" chirruped Doc. "About time you perked up and took a little interest in living. I'm telling you cowboy — you gave us some mighty anxious moments. Four different times I gave you up. But Jean here — say, this girl don't know what it is to cry quits. She insisted that you'd live and by gollies, she was right, all the time. Jean, you can get him a cup of thin broth."

Jean nodded and went out, while Doc peeled back the covers and prodded a bit around Buck's chest and shoulder. "I savvy now," accused Buck weakly. "All the time you were the old devil that kept sticking his cussed fingers into me. I used to cuss that devil."

Doc Pollard laughed. "I had to prod deep, Buck — to get at the lead you were packing. But I got it out."

He covered Buck up again as Jean came in with the broth. She pulled a chair up beside Buck's bed, while Doc turned to examine Johnny Frazier's head.

That broth sure was awful good stuff, especially when you had a swell girl like Jean Harper spooning it between your clumsy lips. Buck got away with all of it and could feel the strength of it creeping through his wasted frame.

"Hate to be such a doggoned baby," he muttered. "Be able to feed myself again one of these days."

She laid a cool, fragrant palm on his lips. "Of course you will," she agreed. "And now — hush! No more talking. Go to sleep again."

She smiled gravely down at him and Buck obediently closed his eyes and drifted off blissfully, thinking how doggoned swell she looked and how soft her hand had been on his lips.

Two weeks later Buck was sitting up in bed and taking on solid food. Doc Pollard had sent old Tony Chavez, the town barber up to the room and Buck was shaved and shorn for the first time in a month. He rubbed a gaunt hand across his smooth chin and decided he wasn't quite such a hatchet faced scarecrow as he had been. Fact of it was, he was feeling like a real human again.

Shortly after the barber left, Bud Tharp came in with Bill Morgan following along on a clumsily handled pair of crutches.

"About time," accused Buck. "You two jiggers would leave a man in this danged hotel to rot before you'd come around and say howdy."

"We'd have been up sooner, only Doc Pollard wouldn't let us," defended Bud. "Hell, man — you don't know how doggoned sick you have been. Four different times they had the grave dug for you and, being the kind of contrary galoot you are, you let 'em do all the work for nothing."

Buck chuckled. "Kick up some chairs and get ready to talk. I got a lot of questions to ask you. Build me a cigarette, like a good guy, Bud. These paws of mine are still a little clumsy."

"Just how much of the story do you know, anyhow, kid?" asked Bill Morgan.

"Well," grunted Buck — "not a hell of a lot. I got things figured out up until the time that last slug hit me. Who threw that one, anyhow?"

"Cutts," said Bud Tharp. "I dropped him cold, the next second."

"How'd you happen into town? Far as I can remember, Johnny and me were the only ones in our crowd who went to town that day."

"You can thank Sam Alstair for that, Buck. Soon as the ruckus broke in town here, Sam forked a bronc and nearly killed it, riding to the Circle Star. He told us that you and Johnny were cornered in Pete Allen's store by the J Bar C, so me and some of the other boys came in ahelling. We didn't get here any too soon."

"I'll buy Sam a drink for that some day,"

Buck nodded. "How are things out on the range?"

"Plenty quiet," Bill Morgan rumbled. "Buck, to all practical intent and purpose, there ain't any more J Bar C. With Jaeger and Cutts dead — you got Jaeger and Whistler Hahn, you know — well, with Jaeger and Cutts out of the picture, the J Bar C is just about folded up."

"That's what we all worked for," muttered Buck grimly. "Any line yet on who killed Judge Henning and Duke Younger?"

"Not for certain. Maybe we never will know. Brood Shotwell — he's coming along fine now — well, Brood figures that maybe Spike St. Ives might have killed the Judge — either him or Toad Black. It's pretty hard to tell who did it. Brood figures that Toad Black might have done for Duke Younger. You remember that it was Younger who first caved and admitted that the jury was bought. And maybe Black killed him because he squealed. Maybe it was Jaeger or Cutts who did the killing of both those men — or ordered it done. You can't tell. Anyway, it was all a mighty dirty mess, and me — I'm shore glad it's over with. I've sprouted a lot of grey hairs in the past three, four months. Tom Addis is shore walking the chalk line. Danged if I don't feel kind of sorry for the old coot."

Buck nodded. "I can sort of understand Tom's position. He was old — and that ranch was all he had — him and Judge Henning being in the same boat. No, I don't hold nothing against Tom Addis. But that whelp, Toad Black — I'm sorry he got away. He tried one trick — the dirtiest of all. I'd feel better —."

"Calm yourself — calm yourself," grunted Bill Morgan. "Don't lose no sleep over that, kid. Toad Black is all done. He made the mistake of trying to get even with Bones Baker — maybe because Bones hit him that lick with the frying pan. It was like this. The day after the big brawl here in town, Bones went out to get an armful of stove wood. Black was hid out up west of the ranchhouse and he cut down on Bones with a Winchester. If Bones hadn't been packing that wood he'd have been plugged square in that fat belly of his. But the wood stopped the slug, though the shock knocked Bones down. He scrambled up and hightailed it for the house, with Black dusting his heels with lead, all the way.

"Mad! Say — old Bones was so mad he foamed. He grabbed that old buffalo Sharps gun of his, sneaked out the other side of the house and got a fair crack at Black as Black was pulling his freight. What that big Sharps slug did to Black was a big plenty. It shore removed that gent from this vale of tears — plumb complete."

Buck grinned. "Good old Bones." Then he sobered. "I reckon money is all right, if it is the right sort of money. But when it is dirty and buys up the honor and souls of men — it's the lowest thing on earth. Call the roll and see what J Bar C money did. Think of the men on both sides, who paid with everything, just because of dirty dollars. Shucks! For a time, back there during that ruckus in the store, I thought they'd got Johnny, too. Reckon we might as well forget all that now, seeing that it's history. But it shore seems good to be square with the world once more, and to know that you got friends."

"Come on, Bill," scoffed Bud Tharp. "We stick around here any longer and that walloper will be weeping all over our shirts. Besides, we got work to do." He leveled a forefinger at Buck. "You better be up and doing yourself, young fellow. Your own cattle are having calves, you know — and Bill and I will be slapping our irons on those slicks if you don't get about taking care of them. Also and besides, your neighbor at the Wineglass, being what you might call a lady tenderfoot, she'll probably be needing some advice on how to run a cow ranch, from an up and coming young gent about your size and complexion."

"You," declared Buck, grinning — "can go plumb to hell."

Bud Tharp cackled his mirth and Bill Morgan guffawed deeply as they went out.

Their departure left Buck restless and, when Doc Pollard dropped in for a couple of minutes later in the day, Buck broached the subject of getting up and forking leather again.

Doc pretended to be horrified. "Take it easy — take it easy, cowboy. You got to learn to walk again before you can ride. Ask me the same question say about ten days or two weeks from now and I might give it a little consideration."

Buck stewed and fumed over this edict and one day when he was alone, tried to get out of bed and show the world that he was just as good as ever. But when he tottered around like a century-old man and nearly fell down two or three times, he decided that maybe Doc did know what he was talking about after all. So he crawled back into bed and was mighty glad to get there.

Came a wonderful day finally, when, on a warm, drowsy morning, Buck Comstock led a pony from the livery barn and swung stiffly into the saddle and reined away from town.

Lord! It sure was good to be in the leather once more, watching a pony's ears bobbing along in front of you. And the old range country, though it was plenty familiar, looked somehow different. Take East and West Buttes for instance. It was funny, thought Buck, that he'd never noticed before how rich the coloring was in them, with that pale violet sun haze swimming about them. And the range itself, all tawny and gold, with the larks awhistling and the bees digging out a winter store of sage honey.

You had to, Buck mused, go way down into the cold depths where old man death leered and grabbed at you, to really appreciate what living really was. You had to fight off all those grisly horrors which infested that pit he'd been sunk in for so long, to really find the meaning in the good old sun and the good old world. You bet. A fellow had to go through all of that, to know that pleasure which was almost like some funny pain — just because you had an honest Visalia saddle between your knees again, with a sturdy, little pony under you, fox-footing it along through the grass and sage. If you had all these things, along with a clear record and sound health once more — then the world was your oyster. Yes sir!

He crossed Timber Valley, where the former J Bar C headquarters stood forlorn and deserted. And he crossed Coyote Valley, stopping only once to watch in huge delight, while a white face cow fondly licked a knobby kneed, shaky legged, new-born little white face bummer. And when the cow bellowed, deep in her throat and eyed Buck suspiciously, he laughed aloud.

"Take that kink out of your tail, old lady," he told the cow. "I'm not going to hurt your pop-eyed darling. The little cuss ain't much to look at now, but he'll make a real beef, one of these days."

In the end he came into the north end of Cotton Valley, where, out there ahead of him the Wineglass ranch buildings stood. There were two punchers working around the corral and Buck recognized them as Dave Wilkins and Hobey Sayre, both former Circle Star riders. They hailed him with broad grins.

"Time you was up and around, you danged old sissy," chuckled Dave Wilkins. "How's it feel to be forking leather once more?"

"Great! How come you boys are working here?"

"Bill Morgan sent us up to sort of keep things moving for Miss Jean until she could get a crew together. Now it looks like Bill had lost two darned good cow nurses. Miss Jean does the cooking around this spread and man — do we eat! Mama!"

Buck built a cigarette. "Where is your new boss, anyhow? I may hit her up for a riding job myself."

"Oh — yeah?" mocked Hobey Sayre skeptically. "You ain't fooling me and Dave — not one little bit. But if you must know, she's up at the house, probably brewing a couple more pies for supper."

"Pie!" exclaimed Buck. "Say, cowboy, I'm a drunkard where pie is concerned. I'm going up and see if I can beg a couple of wedges from her."

He left his pony at the corrals and stalked over to the ranchhouse. He was thinner than he had been, but his step was sure and buoyant and his eyes were clear and bright, filled with a quick eagerness.

The prophecy by Hobey Sayre turned

out to be a good one. Buck found her in the kitchen, her cheeks flushed with the heat of the stove, her hands and bared forearms dusted with flour. She greeted him with a grave, still sweetness.

"I'm glad, Buck," she told him quietly. "Glad to see you up and around again."

"I couldn't hang around that cussed hotel any longer," he told her. "You wouldn't come to see me any more, so I had to come out to you. Why have you stayed away so long, Jean? Soon as Doc was certain I'd get well, you pulled out and I haven't seen you from that day until right here and now."

She met his eyes for a second, then looked away while she became busy over her kitchen table again. "I had a ranch," she murmured. "I had to get out and look after it. Besides," and here her voice became very, very soft — "besides, I knew you could find the trail out here."

Buck moved over and stood beside her. The top of her dark little head came just to his chin. "There's been a lot of water under the bridge, Jean — since I first saw you. A lot of things have been done I wish could have been — otherwise. But Life has a way of sort of throwing things at a person and you just got to climb right over them and keep on moving ahead. There is one thing which I'm wondering if you could ever forget."

She rested her hands flat on the table top and stood very still. "You are still thinking — of Ben Sloan?" she asked.

"Yes. Of Ben Sloan."

"I think we can both forget that, Buck. There was a time when what happened between you — and Ben Sloan — would have filled me with horror. That was before this West of yours had a chance to work on me. Now — it has done something to me. Maybe it has broadened me — maybe it has toughened me. I'm not exactly sure, just which it is. Yet, I do know this. The past is dead, Buck. I'm looking only at the future — and I want — you to look at only that, also."

"Then — ?" said Buck, thinking of that tremendous moment in the Stirrup Cross ranchhouse when she had crept within the circle of his arms, frightened and weeping. "Then — ?"

She glanced straight up at him now and her eyes were deep and soft and glowing clear. "Yes, Buck," she told him bravely.

His arms went about her and she came to him without the slightest hesitation. And after a bit, when her lips were free once more, she burrowed her fragrant head against his shoulder and sighed like a contented child.

"Buck — I thought you never, never would get well enough to ride — the trail — to me."

The employees of Thorndike Press hope you have enjoyed this Large Print book. All our Large Print titles are designed for easy reading, and all our books are made to last. Other Thorndike Press Large Print books are available at your library, through selected bookstores, or directly from us.

For information about titles, please call:

(800) 223-1244
(800) 223-6121

To share your comments, please write:

Publisher
Thorndike Press
295 Kennedy Memorial Drive
Waterville, ME   04901